PENGUIN BOOKS

Rhythm

Rebekah Palmer, 34, was a journalist for many years and now works as a freelance editor and writer. She is based in Wellington with her partner Bernard Steeds and their two children. This is her second novel.

Rhythm

Rebekah Palmer

To Guy,
You've got rhythm!

love

Rebekah

PENGUIN BOOKS

PENGUIN BOOKS

Published by the Penguin Group
Penguin Books (NZ) Ltd, cnr Airborne and Rosedale Roads, Albany,
Auckland 1310, New Zealand
Penguin Books Ltd, 80 Strand, London, WC2R 0RL, England
Penguin Group (USA) Inc., 375 Hudson Street, New York, NY 10014, United States
Penguin Books Australia Ltd, 250 Camberwell Road, Camberwell,
Victoria 3124, Australia
Penguin Books Canada Ltd, 10 Alcorn Avenue, Toronto,
Ontario, Canada M4V 3B2
Penguin Books (South Africa) (Pty) Ltd, 24 Sturdee Avenue, Rosebank,
Johannesburg 2196, South Africa
Penguin Books India (P) Ltd, 11, Community Centre, Panchsheel Park,
New Delhi 110 017, India
Penguin Books Ltd, Registered Offices: 80 Strand, London, WC2R 0RL, England

First published by Penguin Books (NZ) Ltd, 2004

1 3 5 7 9 10 8 6 4 2

Designed by Mary Egan
Typeset by Egan-Reid Ltd
Printed in Australia by McPherson's Printing Group

ISBN 0 14 301905 8

A catalogue record for this book is available
from the National Library of New Zealand.

www. penguin. co. nz

The assistance of Creative New Zealand towards the production
of this book is gratefully acknowledged by the Publisher.

ACKNOWLEDGEMENTS

I gratefully acknowledge the financial assistance of Creative New Zealand and the Todd Foundation. Thank you to my publishers Penguin, especially Geoff Walker. I would like to thank also the invaluable Bernard Steeds, Jane Parkin, Tracey Bridges, Margaret and Geoffrey Palmer, and Geraldine and Malcolm Steeds for their advice, support, encouragement and babysitting services. Thank you to Gwendoline for bringing me such joy in procrastination.

Adrian

Do
Re
Mi
Fa
Sol
La
Si

Michael

Red
Orange
Yellow
Green
Blue
Indigo
Violet

Cara

Allegro
Andante
Stringendo
Ritenuto
Lento
Presto
Tempo primo

Adrian

$\mathcal{D}o$

I REMEMBER the first time I saw Cara. She thinks the first time we met was at her wedding, although we hardly spoke to each other then. But it was actually before that – it was more than a year earlier. Every time I think about that, I see how things could have been so different. It was such an opportunity, lost – wasted, more like. Maybe that was the time we were meant to get together, in some parallel universe. Before Michael, before she got married. Only I blew it. Only I was too shit-scared even to ask her her name.

It was about five years ago now. I was young. I guess I'm still young – younger than Cara anyway. Not that that makes any difference. I'd just turned 24. I remember because it was on the night of my birthday that I broke my arm. I jumped off the big rock at North Beach, must've hit it on the way down. Didn't even notice at the time, I was so pissed. The next morning I woke early, arm swollen like a ham-hock and hurting like hell. The doctor referred me for an X-ray.

I didn't believe in love at first sight back then, not really. Lust at first sight, maybe. But now I think maybe I fell in love as soon as I saw Cara. It sounds too bloody simple. But there was something about her. Something that connected immediately. So I remembered her. As soon as Lissa and I lined up to offer congratulations after the wedding service, I realised she was that woman from the X-ray, and I remembered the feeling.

I'd felt pretty sorry for myself the day we first met. My arm was killing me. And I had some gigs coming up, so I was pissed off. The airhead on reception gave me forms to fill out, even though I'd told her my arm was probably broken. I sat there glaring at the fucking things until someone called my name. I looked up to see a small woman with a pointed face. Cara. She was wearing a white tunic over black trousers, her thick brown hair pulled back in a ponytail, so she looked about my age. She took the blank forms from me.

'Arm, is it? Sorry, the receptionist is a bit of a blonde. Come through and I'll fill them in for you.'

We went through to a radiography room and she asked me my details, writing in a quick, neat hand.

'And how did it happen?'

I mumbled. 'It was my birthday yesterday.'

'Say no more. Drunk as a skunk, no doubt.'

I remember her hair, her eyes. She was beautiful, all

right. Maybe it would have been different if she hadn't been so attractive. Beautiful women always make me feel inadequate. She had long chestnut hair, which glinted gold, thick and rich, as if it had just been brushed. I wanted to touch its glossiness, reach out and put my fingers through it.

'The X-ray's just a formality really.'

'You think it's broken then?'

'Almost certainly. My bet is you'll be in a cast for the next six weeks.'

'Shit.'

'Exams coming up?'

'Gigs. I'm a drummer.'

'Yeah? Cool. I always wanted to have a go at that.'

That was my chance. The universe had set it all up for me. That's when I should have said, 'Come along, here's some free tickets.' Instead, I looked into those big brown eyes, just looked and looked, and the phone rang. Fuck it.

♪ ♪ ♪

The next time we met was at her wedding. I recognised her as soon as we got up close and Lissa introduced us. They were old school friends; Lissa and I had only been going out six weeks or so. Of course now Lissa thoroughly disapproves of me. She found out what happened and wrote me a letter, if you can call it that. 'You prick,' she said. 'I can't believe I introduced you to her.'

I noticed it again on the wedding day, put it down to the inevitable brilliance of a bride. There's always something special about a bride, they say. So that's what I thought it was. Until the next time we met and there, again, she was just as . . . luminous.

Cara would laugh at the word, but it describes her well. Luminous. She had this light about her that drew me in. A moth. A great hairy moth beating senselessly against a hard glass lampshade. Drawn by the brilliance of the light. Because it can't do anything else but seek that light, endlessly, until it is consumed by it.

It sounds ridiculous now, even to me. But at the time it was so strong and sure. I wanted nothing but to be with her. She filled my whole vision; the sound of her voice made me deaf to all else. I was intent on her. Some people (Michael) would argue that you can't force love, that it either comes of its own accord or it doesn't. Crap. There's always the seeds of potential, and if you know how to cultivate it that potential can grow and flourish – and what do you know, just give her a little push and she thinks she's falling, falling, and there's a sudden rush and she turns her head towards you like the sun and you witness the flowering.

That makes me sound cynical. I wasn't cynical, not about her. It was just that I wanted her so much. I would do anything to make her want me.

♪ ♪ ♪

It was almost a year after the wedding that Cara and I met again. Lissa brought her to a Pulse show one night. I'd asked her to, actually. Lissa had mentioned Cara in passing and I said, 'Why don't you bring her along some time?' I don't remember the show much. It was one of the active ones, before we got into the softer stuff, and there was lots of running around on stage. It was a good show, high energy, but Pulse has come a long way since then. We thought we were avant-garde at the time. We were doing a range of drum dances, using everyday stuff – hubcaps, sticks, pots and pans. I'd just written *Delta*, the one with the water fountains, and we were performing that for the first time. It seems a long time ago now. I'm not into that stuff any more.

I remember Lissa was pregnant. She looked good though. That glowing thing. I always think pregnant women look sexy. I said something about it once to Lissa and she said that was typical of me – I always wanted women who were obviously taken – but that's not it. Apparently there's a stage pregnant women go through where they feel really horny; that must show through, I reckon.

Anyway, that night I wasn't paying much attention to Lissa; it was Cara I was watching. It wasn't even anything she did. I came into the café after the show and saw her sitting there with Liss, and right then I wanted to know who she was, what music she liked, what was her favourite colour, what she thought of it all. Lissa was a bit of an impediment, but Pete came and picked her up shortly afterwards, so we were alone. We sat at my favourite table in the corner by the window, and I offered to get her some cake with her coffee. She shook her head in a bashful way.

'I'm watching my figure.'

'So am I, and there's nothing wrong with it from where I'm sitting.'

'Women always worry about their weight.'

'Even when you've got the perfect body?'

'I should imagine so,' she said. 'It's the guilt.'

'I don't believe in guilt.'

'Perhaps you should eat the cake then.'

'Let's have half each. Then we can be guilty together.'

Gradually she warmed up and I took my foot off the gas a bit. We even talked about her wedding. Then we got on to music and she asked me about my composing.

'I seem to be in a performance-only phase at the moment,' I said. 'I'm missing something I need for it.'

'What do you need for it?'

I wasn't sure what to say. I needed space, I needed inspiration, I needed to believe in something. I looked up at her face – serious, waiting for me to reply. Her hair was pulled back and her cheeks faintly flushed. She was so . . . interested. That's when I first felt that fluttering, so soft, like a butterfly, so soft I scarcely noticed.

'What do you need?' she repeated.

'Faith,' I said.

It felt like we shared a secret from then on. I relaxed, was much less careful, less calculating. I said what I thought, on the whole. And it worked. She liked me, the real me. I could tell, because she liked my music. *Delta*

16

was her favourite piece in the show, she said, entirely unprompted. You could always tell Cara meant what she said. She was very . . . genuine.

Was it that night I fell in love with her? Is it possible to pinpoint the moment like that? It did feel different after that night. I wasn't just trying to get her into bed. I asked her for a lift home. I even kissed her. But I didn't expect anything of it; I knew her already. I knew I was in for the long haul.

♪ ♪ ♪

I rang her a few days later.

'Cara, it's Adrian.'

'Oh, hello.' She sounded like she was feigning surprise, but she was pleased too. I delayed, let her wonder what I wanted.

'How are you?' she asked.

'I'm fine. I was wondering if maybe I left my wallet in your car. I seem to have lost it.'

'Oh, well, I haven't found it. Hang on, I'll go look.'

I knew it was under the seat.

'Yes, it's here. I'll drop it round to you.'

'Don't worry. I'll come and pick it up. Are you going to be at work around lunchtime?'

'Actually I'm going to be at home. Would you like to come for lunch?'

Perfect. So I went round there for lunch. Very casual.

The house was 'nice'. It wasn't my taste, but it was done up with some style. A suburban bungalow, but bright and quirky, like Cara. They had some good art; I spotted a few originals in the hallway. They were doing all right for themselves.

We went into the kitchen. It had a commercial gas oven with a huge rangehood backed by a mosaic of Italian tiles, and there was a wooden island in the middle of the room. The sun streamed in through a wall of windows set around a large pair of glass doors.

'Who's the cook?'

'Me, I guess.'

'Sounds promising.'

'Not really. There's leftovers. Like some wine?'

We went through the glass doors and sat at a picnic table on the deck. Cara poured a couple of glasses of riesling.

'Here's to . . .' She paused. 'Here's to what?'

'Here's to you,' I said.

It wasn't as easy as that, of course. That was simply the beginning. I wasn't counting on anything. I never took anything for granted, especially Cara.

'How long have you lived here?'

'About three years.'

'Looks like a good house for children.'

She laughed and I almost fell off my chair. Her laugh was like music. She didn't laugh much, didn't even smile very often, but it was worth it when she did.

'That's what Lissa says,' she said. 'She wants to buy it from us.'

'Do you want to have children?'

It pays to check this one out early.

18

'I guess, one day. I know Michael wants children.'

'You sound like you're not so sure.'

'Well, I don't know.' She fiddled with the stem of her wine glass, took another sip. 'I'm not sure I'm ready to be responsible for somebody else.'

I wasn't fooled. I can always recognise that state in women: that state where they need to have children. Cara wasn't there yet, but she wouldn't be long. I could see that already. All the women I've known have either got children, want children or are about to want children. I don't think I've ever met a woman who doesn't want to have children. I suppose they exist. But even if they say they don't, I find they generally do, eventually. I always lose interest in women once they reach that point. I can't help it. They begin to remind me of my mother, and that's always the death-knell. You can't fancy your own mother. That's just sick.

If there was anyone Cara reminded me of then, it was me. The old me: how I used to be before I started doing what I wanted to do, before I started playing drums for a living. Lost.

'I don't really like this house,' she said. 'Michael does, though, and I couldn't think of a reason not to buy it, so I went along with it.'

'You could always change it.'

'We already have. The kitchen, anyway. I had to have a good kitchen.'

'I can see why. If these are leftovers, the real thing must have been a knock-out.'

'I was going to be a chef once, but I wasn't confident

19

enough, and radiography had better hours. Besides, I was afraid cooking all the time would destroy my love for it. Do you find that with drumming? Do you get bored practising?'

'I don't do enough of it to get bored.'

'Don't you practise much?'

'I never practise.'

'You *never* practise?'

'No, I play.'

'Oh.'

She looked at me with this gleam in her eye, as if she'd just realised something. It was the gleam that got me. I wanted to see it again and again. I wanted to see it turn into something more. Once she got going, you could see that Cara would really be someone. She could be anyone she wanted, once she found her rhythm. I wanted to help her find it. That was how it all started.

♪ ♪ ♪

Re

I WOKE up the next morning hearing her laugh. I was shocked awake, convinced that Cara was in the room. I sat up and looked all around, my breath fast and jagged, certain I'd see her small form sitting on the end of my bed. But there was just the thin curtain flapping in the morning breeze. I must have left the window open. I lay down again and drew the sheet up over my cold skin, and crossed my hands against my chest. After a while my breathing slowed. I listened to it, soft and quiet, felt the air's slight warmth against my face. I closed my eyes, and the little sounds – my breathing, a bird outside, the faint buzz of my stereo left on but not playing – all the little sounds fell away and I heard the silence surrounding. Then after a minute I heard a new sound, steady, regular, soothing, and I felt the vibrations against my hand. Bom,

bom. Bom, bom. Bom, bom. Bom, bom. My heartbeat. I lay listening to it for ages, until I fell asleep.

I had to see her again, but I didn't know how. I went over to Lissa's. She was in a foul mood, in her last days of pregnancy. I raised the subject as soon as I practically could.

'So tell me about Cara.'

'Cara? What do you want to know? She's a radiographer, about my age, loves French films, is a great cook and is *married*.'

I smiled in what I thought was a wry fashion.

'I knew it!' Lissa exclaimed. 'I knew it when I saw you kiss her hand at the café. You bastard.'

'Curious, merely curious.'

'She's not one of your conquests, Adrian. She's one of my friends. And she's happily married.'

'What do you mean "one of my conquests"? For fuck's sake.'

'I know you. I know you only too well.'

I sometimes forget I used to go out with Lissa. I don't usually stay friends with old girlfriends.

'I was just asking, all right.'

'Well, don't.'

I was surprised by her tone and tried to play it down a little.

'She just seemed . . . nice.'

'Yeah, well she is. Too nice for you.'

'Okay, okay. Happily married. Got it.'

'Hasn't stopped you before. Adrian.'

She paused and put down the washing she was folding,

lots of teeny pink baby things, and came round the other side of the table to me. I felt slightly alarmed. She stood there with her hands on her hips, pregnant belly pointed at me accusingly.

'You're huge,' I said.

'Adrian. Promise me you won't.'

'Won't what?'

'You know what.'

'All right, all right. Jesus. Remind me never to cross a pregnant woman.'

She smiled weakly and sat down at the table.

'And you can finish folding that bloody washing,' she said.

♪ ♪ ♪

Lissa rang me later that afternoon.

'I just wanted to apologise.'

'What for?'

'I might have come across a little strong today. Hormones, you know.'

'Sounds like a good excuse to me.'

'It's not an excuse. It's a reason.'

'Okay, sure, whatever.'

'I think I was just projecting, you know? Because of the way our relationship ended.'

'You always were a little paranoid.'

'Fuck you Adrian.'

'Any time darlin'. Just get rid of the basketball first, eh?'

Luckily, she laughed.

♪ ♪ ♪

About a week later I heard from Pete that the baby had arrived.

'I'll just rush round with my hand-knitted booties then.'

'On ya. Actually, a curry would be more appreciated. We're doing visitors between 10 and 12.'

'What is this? I have to book in?'

'Babies are in hot demand. The two grandmas are coming today, and Cara's coming tomorrow. You'll be lucky if we can fit you in towards the end of the week.'

'Bet you're dying to go back to work.'

I just happened to drop in between 10 and 12 the next day. I even picked up a curry. Lissa was quite touched. I almost felt guilty.

'You are a honey. Come in and meet Ellie. We've already got some visitors.'

Visitors. Plural. Michael.

I followed Liss into the living-room a little reluctantly. I hadn't prepared for this. But sitting on the couch, tea perched on her knee, was Cecily, another friend of Lissa's. I scanned the room and saw Cara standing by the windows. No Michael. I relaxed.

'Pete taken the babe out then?' I asked.

'As unobservant as usual,' said Liss. 'I'm just going to the loo. Back in a tick.'

Cara turned from the window, her long hair swishing

like the tail of a horse. She raised her slender eyebrows in greeting. 'Here,' she said, holding up the pile of blankets awkwardly. There was a tiny, pink, wrinkled face set in the middle of the whiteness. I almost stepped back in shock.

'Jesus.'

Cara giggled. 'Don't let Liss hear you.'

'I brought a curry,' I said stupidly.

The baby started to squeak. Cara panicked and thrust it towards me.

'You take her.'

'Me? No way.'

Cecily got up from the couch, calmly took the bundle and walked around the room, shush-shushing like a gentle wind until the squeaking stopped.

'Thank God for that,' Cara whispered to me. 'I'm completely incompetent with babies.'

Her face was flushed and her eyes sparkled. Still in with a chance, I thought. I felt high and stupid. Lissa came back and scarcely noticed us, went straight to the baby and began discussing the intricacies of breast-feeding with Cecily, who had twins. Cara and I stayed over by the windows, looking out over the garden.

'How's the music?' she asked.

I liked that. Most people didn't ask, and if they did, they didn't call it music.

'Good. We're going away on tour soon.'

'Where?'

'Everywhere. Small towns mainly.'

'Great. How long for?'

'Six weeks.'

Six weeks without seeing her.

'Tours must be fun.'

'I hate them. It's not like you get to see anywhere. We're always on the road, or in some hole of a hotel, and the food sucks.'

She shrugged in a sympathetic fashion.

'What about the drugs and groupies?'

'What about them?'

'Oh. I was joking actually.'

'So was I,' I said quickly.

Lissa was waving something about that looked like a plastic nipple. My legs felt hot and itchy. Why had I worn woollen trousers?

'I better get going.'

I couldn't move.

'Have a good tour then.'

Cecily was leaving now and Lissa showed her to the door. I felt a trickle of sweat on the back of my knee. Cara was looking at me.

'Do you know you X-rayed my arm once?' I said. Fuckin' idiot.

'Really? I don't remember.'

Lissa came back and set the baby down in a bassinet in the corner of the room.

'She's asleep, thank God.'

'I've got to go,' I said.

'Me too,' said Cara, getting her bag from behind the couch.

I made myself walk over to Lissa. I had to get out of

there. I was itching all over.

'I'll see you in October. We're off on tour in a couple of weeks.'

'I suppose you don't want our season tickets for the symphony orchestra, then? I get the feeling we won't be using them.'

'I usually get freebies anyway.'

'I forgot. You're one of the in-crowd. How about you, Cara?'

'I'd love them. But I doubt if Michael would be interested.'

'So? Go on your own,' said Liss.

The phone rang. 'Shit.' She rushed into the hall to stifle it.

'I'll go with you, if you like,' I said.

Cara's eyes flickered.

'But aren't you on tour?'

'Not for another two weeks or so. We could go Saturday.'

'Sure. That'd be great.'

♪ ♪ ♪

I always think of that night as our first date. We had arranged to meet in the bar half an hour before the concert. She was 20 minutes late. By that time I was convinced she wasn't coming and I'd just ordered my third drink. It's amazing how quickly your mood can change, just from the simple sight of a face. It felt like a reprieve from a sentence.

Her face was pale, not much make-up, a little mascara, a light brown lipstick. Her hair was out, hanging loosely round her shoulders like a mane. She was taking off a scarlet scarf that set off the red in her hair, and frowning, a cross little line between her eyes.

'I'm so sorry,' she said. 'It's Michael's fault.'

I liked it being Michael's fault. At least, I liked that she was angry with him. The fact that he could determine her movements, wield such influence, I didn't like. He got to do all the everyday things with her – see her in her dressing gown at breakfast, share a bathroom with her, watch TV with her, drop her off to meet a friend, late. I was deeply envious.

It was a mixed programme. The only piece I remember is the 1812 Overture because, as the tympani mimicked the cannons at the end, Cara reached over and squeezed my hand. Her perfume was fruity, sweet. I sniffed it in and saliva flooded my mouth. Later, that scent would always have the same effect. I'd catch it passing a woman on the street and turn, my mouth flooded, and have to blink. I never could listen to that bloody Overture again.

Besides love, besides that ridiculous passion that rose in my veins every time I saw Cara, it was anger I felt most those days. Another emotion that runs in the blood. It would flare at just as odd times. You'd think I would have been angry most when she was talking about Michael. Like when we had a drink after the concert at the hotel bar across the road. I didn't mean to take her to a hotel, it happened to be the closest, and the quietest on a Saturday night in town. There were only a handful of

28

people there. We sat by the windows on a large green leather couch, munching peanuts, our beers on the low coffee table before us.

'You're very beautiful.'

She looked startled.

'What?'

'It's the peanuts.' I held one up and wiggled it.

'What are you talking about?'

'They're complimentary.'

Such an idiot. But she laughed. A couple sitting a few tables away looked over: she had such a lovely, strong laugh. If you looked at her closely while she laughed, you could see a gap between her two front teeth. I think that might be why she didn't laugh or smile so much. Sometimes I'd see her put her hand over her mouth as if she was hiding a smile. I wished she wouldn't. I found the gap endearing, the flaw proof of her loveliness.

'That's the worst joke I ever heard. Worse even than Michael's jokes. And Michael's jokes are pretty bad.'

'You don't often hear of funny psychiatrists.'

'It's because he doesn't really get them. He'll start telling a joke and then halfway through he'll forget how it ends because he never really got it in the first place, so he's forgotten why it's funny. So you get this joke where the punch-line isn't quite right and you go, "What? What's that about?", and there's Michael, roaring with laughter.'

She laughed again, and I laughed with her. I could have felt angry then, resentful of her fondness for the man. But it didn't even touch me. I didn't usually get angry when she talked about Michael. It was only afterwards – when I was alone, thinking of him being with her – the anger came. And occasionally, very occasionally, it would come when we were together. Usually I was too wrapped up in the experience to connect with those feelings. But sometimes it would boil over out of nowhere. Like the night we went dancing, just before I left on tour.

We'd been having a good time. We went to a movie, then met up with a group of people at a club, and we were both pretty relaxed – I don't know about her but I was usually more relaxed when there were others around us. We were drinking a lot; I was trying to slow my pace, but Cara was definitely drinking more than usual. It was good dancing with her. She wasn't a great dancer – she held herself too tightly for that, although the drink helped her loosen up. But it felt good to be able to be with her and not have to talk, to be able just to watch her. She was so beautiful.

And it became much more than her looks. It was her gestures: the way her long, slender fingers stroked the air when she was trying to describe something. It was the things she said. I listened to everything she said, every little thing. I probably put too much into it. I guess I could have misconstrued some things. I imagined we were talking in a private code half the time. I'd say things, ambiguous things, and I knew she would know what they meant. I'd puzzle over her replies in turn, sometimes exulted when they confirmed she knew. She was so clever at saying the exact right thing in reply. I still replay those conversations. But now I'm not so sure of the meaning. Did she know? Were we playing the same game? Maybe it wasn't a game at all.

By the end of the evening she was definitely drunk. Most of the group I knew had left by then; two or three were still dancing. Cara and I sat together on one of the small couches, close, touching, her bare arms warm and her stone bracelet cold against my skin. It felt like something could happen. She leaned her head against my shoulder and looked up at me, her eyelids half closed.

'I need to go to bed,' she said, looking right at me. She didn't say it but I felt the words: 'Are you coming?' And suddenly I was angry. Not like this, it wasn't meant to happen like this, so easily. I could hardly look at her. I stood up and pulled her up roughly by one hand.

'Come on. Let's get you home.'

Stupid tart, I thought. Why did you have to ruin it?

I don't know why I was so angry. Wasn't that what I wanted?

I put her in a taxi and walked all the way home. I was sober by the time I arrived, and the dawn was breaking. I watched the sun come over the hills, the morning light so bright, so clear. I thought of her sleeping, lying next to Michael, and I wanted to be with her. The anger evaporated. As quickly as it had arrived. I don't know why. Anger comes from fear, I guess. Where does love come from?

♪ ♪ ♪

Mi

IT WAS bad timing, that tour. Three main centres, plus eight other towns. Six weeks without even the chance of seeing Cara.

Timing is important. Everything has its own time and you have to get it right. If you miss the right time for something, that's it. There may be another time but it will be different then. Like in music. There's the beat and there's the spaces around the beat and everything has its place. One is just as important as the other, and if the timing of one is altered, so everything is changed. It's a living thing. It can always surprise you.

Cara could always surprise me too. The day before we left, she turned up at the end of the rehearsal. She'd brought a big hamper of pies and cake and stuff.

'Thought you could do with some road food.'

'Excellent,' said JJ, taking the basket. 'Wanna come with us? You could be the official chef.'

She smiled one of her rare smiles.

'I don't think you boys could afford me.'

I was packing up the drums and Cara offered to help. The others took off. I put away the bass drums and showed her how to pack up the ashiko and Egyptian dombeq. She paused for a while before a big standing drum, running her fingers over the skin.

'Go on,' I said. 'Give it a whack.'

'That's your technique? Give it a whack? And you call yourself a professional.'

Her eyes were shining and I could see she wanted to have a go. She was stroking the skin with one hand while the other fiddled with the side straps.

'There's no one else here,' I said. 'Go on.'

She looked around as if doubting me, and giggled, a little nervously. I went over to another of the tall African drums and played a couple of strokes.

'Like that.'

She was still uncertain, like I was asking her to ride a horse. Her hand hovered.

'There's a big note in the middle of the head,' I said. 'It's a large drum, so you use your whole hand – thumb, little finger, from your fingertips down to the heel. Make sure you don't curve your hand and don't hit with a lot of force.'

She hit it. It wasn't bad for a first note.

'Now hit it after me.'

I struck the low note again on my drum and she hit

hers, and I led her on until she gained more confidence and the deep note began to ring out. Then, with the other hand, I hit the edge of the drumhead for the high note. Ping. Ping. She got that one almost straight off. I showed her the simplest rhythm using the two notes: bom, ping, bom, ping, bom, ping, bom, ping, nice and steady. It felt strange playing with her. She was still a bit nervous, and frowning a little, concentrating. But she was starting to find it. She played along with me on the tall standing drum, and began to sway slightly with the beat. Then suddenly she got scared and I could see her head come back and she lost it. I stopped too and made light of it. It was a beginning.

♪ ♪ ♪

The tour was the worst yet. I couldn't hide my mood. The first town, I refused to check out the venue with the others and walked on to the hotel. It was one of those ugly small towns, wide streets lined with drooping trees and box houses, half the shops in the main street empty, and kids hanging round with skateboards and blank-eyed stares. The whole place simmered with despair. Or maybe it was just me.

JJ had given me careful instructions on how to get to our hotel, but you couldn't miss it. It was the only one in town, a glorified pub on the corner of the main inter-section. Any remnants of charm had checked out years ago. In the lobby, broken chandeliers hung drunkenly from the ceiling. The net curtains had giant moth holes, and the faded red and gold carpet smelt of beer and cigarettes. Everything was coated with a fine layer of dust.

Despite this, the old trout on the front desk warned me of severe consequences for smoking in the rooms.

'Are you a band?' she asked, peering over her ancient glasses as I filled out the registration forms.

'No ma'am,' I said. 'We're a contemporary percussion ensemble.'

She grunted suspiciously but said no more.

The guys had taken the drums straight to the venue. Shame. I could have done with a bit of drumming. I went up to my room, a cramped cupboard with no bathroom and a tiny window above head height. There was nothing in it but a hard, single bed, a bedside table and a rickety chair. I lay down on the candlewick bedspread. It reeked of cat's piss.

'Fan-fuckin-tastic.'

I pulled off the bedspread and shoved it under the bed, lit up a cigarette and stared at the grey walls for a while, smoking, before lying down again and going to sleep.

♪ ♪ ♪

'Hey Ade. Time to check out the local establishments.'

It was Jimmy, banging on the door. I lifted my head and peered into the half-light. I was in a hotel room. Something smelled foul. The bloody bedspread.

'I'll catch you up.'

'You still in a shit, man? Garn, come for a drink.'

I heard Andy join him.

'What's up?'

'He's packing a sad.'

'Aw, did Adrian want to stay with his girlie?'

I should never have told the prick.

'Piss off. She's not my girlie.'

'Come on mate. There's fresh talent to be had, ready and willing.'

'I said no.'

After they left, I took the bedspread and dumped it in the hallway, and went for a slash. The face in the mirror already looked haggard. I needed to eat. We'd finished Cara's hamper for lunch. Across the road from the hotel was a burger bar. Just the dull-eyed owner waiting patiently behind the greasy counter and a little shit playing the video game. I ordered a burger and chips and ate them in the doorway, watching a few people drift aimlessly down the darkened street, the tinny sound of the video game's hostage drama playing out behind me.

Walking down the main street afterwards, I looked through the windows of McGill's Alehouse and saw the guys chatting up some of the local slags, their table cluttered with empties. I didn't feel like joining them. I went back to the hotel and watched some television in what passed for the lounge before going to bed. Andy banged on my door again about 2 a.m. to wish me a good night's sleep. He obviously hadn't scored.

It wasn't that the guys didn't take the tour seriously – they did. Everyone was always keyed up just before a show. It was just their way of releasing tension. It was my way too, usually. A drink or two never did any harm. It was good to be relaxed when you played. Not like Michael's theory. Cara told me he's convinced drummers are tense and angry people – all that 'violence'. Bollocks. He's assuming there's a lot of force exerted, but there's not. That's just macho bullshit. You've got to be relaxed to play fast patterns for any length of time. Otherwise you burn up the energy reserves too soon. Of course, you can overdo it – too loose and you lose the beat. It's a question of balance. Get the right balance of tension and relaxation in your wrists, you get the right tone. Michael doesn't know shit.

I went out early the next morning before the others got up. Trouble was, there was nowhere to go. I'd seen it all already. I walked past the three blocks of shops, and came to a side street with a sign pointing to the beach. I wondered how long the walk was and half-heartedly started down the road. The moon hung in a crescent in the pale blue sky. I always find it eerie seeing the moon in the daytime.

Houses began to thin after a while, replaced by fields of vegetables, lettuces, potatoes, corn. Closer to the beach, little houses started to appear again, run-down shacks, mostly closed up, but the odd one had someone living there, dogs barking angrily at me through the front gate. It took me 40 minutes to reach the beachfront shops. There were three of them: a dairy, a fish and chip shop, and a laundromat, all closed. An old-fashioned red phone-box stood next to a wooden picnic table outside the dairy. I stood on the table to look over to the sea. It wasn't even that nice a beach. It was one of those wild ones with grey sand and forbidding sand hills snaked with a creek running down to the sea. Now I was here I didn't even want to go onto the beach. The wind got up and I folded my arms across my thin sweatshirt and wished I'd had something to eat.

That must have been the problem: I go a bit mental on an empty stomach. I don't know why else I would've done it. It was a fuckin' stupid thing to do. I guess I didn't even think it would work. You need those phone cards everywhere else. Who would have thought a lousy coin would give me a dial tone?

She answered. That voice. She had quite a deep voice. I bet she could sing. I closed my eyes and tried to picture her picking up the phone in the kitchen, halfway through breakfast – what would she eat for breakfast? Something healthy, grapefruit maybe, some God-awful muesli and yoghurt. Michael reading the paper in the background. Or maybe she was still in bed, maybe they were still in bed . . .

'Hello, hello? I can't hear you?'

What could I say? It was fuckin' stupid. I just stood there.

'Who is this?'

I hung up.

♪ ♪ ♪

The others had almost finished a brunch fry-up when I got back to the hotel. The hotel restaurant smelt of oily eggs and burnt toast. I sat down and scraped up the dregs onto a plate.

'Where've you been?'

'Beach.'

'Yeah, what's it like?'

'Cold.'

'Yeah, I vote for our next tour being in summer,' said JJ.

'No one's home in summer,' said Andy.

'Well, where are they? Let's go where they are. Let's go to beaches and the campgrounds. It'd be a lot more fun than this dive.'

'Anywhere would be more fun than this dive,' I said.

'Jesus, guys. It's only our first gig.'

Andy got up and stalked away.

The eggs slid against the edge of my plate in a pool of yellowy oil, and the bacon was so burnt you couldn't tell what was rind and what was meat.

'Yeah, guys,' I said. 'Look, we get the best food, the best hotels. What are you complaining about?'

The others got up and left too. I sat alone in the dining room and ate. It was going to be one of those tours. There was always someone who was a right pain in the arse. This time it was me.

♪ ♪ ♪

Just before we went on stage that night, Andy took me by the arm.

'Got something to cheer you up.'

He pointed into the audience.

'See the blonde in the middle table at the front? She's yours.'

'What?'

'Yours for the evening. A lovely pussy cat to curl up with. That'll make you forget your brunette back home.'

He bounded up on stage behind Jimmy before I could hit him.

I played differently that night. I was pissed off. Maybe Michael was right: drumming can be angry. The Dance of Shiva – Creation and Destruction. I was bent on destruction that night. I worked up a real sweat. I had fast hot licks, sweet as. It's addictive, that power. I don't usually go there. I was a bit embarrassed afterwards at the others' reactions. They were actually impressed.

'You're playing great,' JJ said to me at the interval.

Andy grinned. 'Got something to look forward to, haven't you mate?'

I went out for some fresh air. I don't know why it upset me so much. Andy was just a dick. I knew that. He'd always been like that. Usually I would have joked with him, played along. But this tour seemed different. I didn't want to be with them. I wanted to be on my own, to be back with Cara. But there was nothing I could do. I was here and she was with Michael. I decided to put it into the drumming, but not anger this time. I needed to stay away from that.

The second half I deliberately avoided the solos. I took over the down-beat and concentrated on consistency. The hardest job in the group is the simplest – that constant repetition. But that's the one beat that's needed. Someone has to hold down the bottom while the others play the rhythm. Usually someone gets excited and plays on top, solos away and doesn't give a damn, caught up in it all. Soloing's great when you're into it – you weave all over, in, around, on top of the groove, like a bird flying through the trees in a forest. But eventually it gets top-heavy, with more people soloing than supporting. That's when it collapses and we all stumble to a close.

Someone's got to take charge, re-establish a different beat for everyone to set to, and if that works we all come back together again. You can tell when you're there, because everyone smiles at each other. Can't get enough of it. Like love.

Like love. Addictive. You get that in drumming too, sometimes. People think you're flakey if you talk about it, but it's true. It's like going into some kind of trance – you just go for it, you hear the beat, beat, beat, and you go into automatic, you're not thinking about it, you're not thinking of anything, it could have been going an hour, a day, it could go on for ever. It's better than drugs, better than sex. Well, maybe not sex.

Anyway, that's what it was like that night. I just coasted along with the rhythm. After a while I forgot about being angry or sad or happy, whatever. I was just there, drumming. Most people don't know what that's like. It's not just me, though. Jimmy came up to me afterwards when we were in the bar and handed me a drink.

'Hey,' he said. 'Were you there, man?'

I nodded and we clinked pints and drank. We didn't even need to talk about it. Andy and JJ don't know that place. Andy tends to play outward to the world, to identify with the thunder and lightning; he likes to feel his body exerting that power. And he's got a real problem speeding up. JJ, he's playing more to, like, impress himself. Underneath, I think he's actually scared. Some people fear the groove: they fight against it, won't surrender. Everyone plays different. I kept wondering what Cara would play like, if she really got going some time. Would she be able to let go?

I looked over at Andy and the blonde. I'd told him he could have her and she didn't seem to have a problem with that. She was all over him. It wasn't any different from any other tour. Except this time I'd grown up. I was in love. There went my chances of enjoying simple lust again. That must have been why I was so angry.

♪ ♪ ♪

Fa

WHEN WE finally got back from the tour, it was another 10 days before I got the chance to see Cara again. I didn't have to arrange a pretence this time – it was Lissa and Pete's wedding anniversary and they invited a few friends to stay at their beach house for the weekend.

I couldn't help asking Lissa.

'Is Cara coming?'

She rolled her eyes at me. 'Why?'

'Why not?'

'Yes, she's coming, and so is Michael.'

'Good,' I said. 'I'll be there.'

I made sure I got there earlier than the others. I don't know why – I just wanted to be ready, to be settled, so when I saw her I wasn't surprised or anything. It didn't even matter that Michael would be there. In fact, I was looking forward to seeing him again. I hadn't really met him at the wedding and this way I'd be able to check him out properly.

Lissa gave me a hug and a martini when I arrived and showed me to a small bare room on the ground floor.

'Single bed, darling.'

'Yes, Mum.'

'The bathroom's by the back door and I'm in the kitchen. Make yourself at home.'

The plan was to be settled. I wasn't. I lay on the bed for a minute, then got up and walked round the room. It took three paces. I went to find Peter. He was in the lounge, feeding the baby a bottle.

'Hey Pete.'

'Here's your Uncle Adrian, Ellie.'

'Hello smelly Ellie.'

'She's not, is she?' He actually sniffed her rear end.

'When are the others arriving?'

'Who knows? Any time after 11, I guess.'

'What is it now?'

'10.15.'

'I might go check out the beach.'

'Go out the back gate and walk 100 metres. You can't miss it. It's the big sandy thing with the wet bit.'

I thought a walk might help calm me down. But there were a few others on the beach, so I went and stood by the waterline and watched the waves wash in and out, in and out. I was like a tense string vibrating.

I realised she might not be as I remembered anyway. People change in your memory. You don't see them for a while, and the things you remember about them you think are the typical things, but maybe they aren't. Maybe they're the atypical things and that's why you remember them. I closed my eyes and thought about what I remembered about Cara.

It was strange. I remembered her voice more than her face. She had a low, rich voice. The kind you hear on radio, a movie-star kind of voice. It went up and down and round your head, as if the words were notes. That first night we'd gone out, I kept losing the gist of what she was saying, simply because I was listening to her voice, the promise it held. That's what I remembered – the promise.

I checked my watch: five to. I didn't want her to arrive just yet. I was sure it would be a disappointment. Only seven weeks since I last saw her, but already she had grown too much in my mind; she had turned into someone else. She'd be bound to fall short of my image of her. It wouldn't be her fault. I convinced myself she would be plain and dull. Then I could be free of this stupidity. I walked back to the beach house.

The Frewens had turned up but not Cara. We all sat out on the porch for a while, drinking. Maybe it was the sun, but two beers seemed to go straight to my head and I couldn't concentrate on what people were saying. I just nodded and smiled at them, kind of humming something under my breath. I felt like composing again. I hadn't felt that way for ages, but I couldn't go off and do it then. She could arrive at any moment. I needed to sober up. I went into the kitchen to get some water. Lissa asked me to

47

squeeze some grapefruit for her.

'You okay?' she asked.

'Yeah, just a bit of a headache. It's too hot. Where's your squeezer?'

'On the shelf there.'

I caught her looking at me. I didn't like it.

'Sure you're okay? There's panadol in the bathroom if you need any,' she said.

'I'll be fine.'

I started slicing the golden fruit.

'You will be, you know,' Lissa said, her hand on my shoulder. 'These things pass.'

I refused to look up. I refused to ask her what she meant. The large knife was sharp and split the fruit in halves with a satisfying slice. The chopping distracted me so I didn't hear the car pull up and missed seeing Cara arrive after all.

'That must be them,' Lissa said.

I almost sliced a finger off.

'Who?' I said.

'Who do you think, ning-nong.' She was arranging a jug and glasses on a tray. 'Fill this with juice and take it outside.'

I fiddled about for a while, then finally grabbed the tray and went. I saw Cara from the doorway and stumbled over on to the deck in front of her, holding the tray up idiotically.

'Hi. Juice?'

Great entrance, dickhead.

She was smiling. I smiled back, then looked around for

the good-looking husband.

'Where's Michael?' asked Liss.

'He got held up. He's coming later tonight.'

Cara went inside with Lissa and I finished offering around the juice. I sat down in the shade and leaned back, closed my eyes for a bit. She'd been wearing a plain white dress. But she wasn't plain. Maybe she would be dull. I almost giggled.

Ridiculous. It all sounds so ridiculous. I could never tell anyone about it for that reason. It's easy enough to talk about sorrow and get away with it. If I was pathetically depressed and sorry for myself, people might take me seriously. But love. How could I explain love? How could I show anyone how *much* I was feeling? How could I give even a taste of the ache, a touch of the excitement that ran through me like an electric current?

Cara was my own private drug. When I was around her I was on a high. I walked around in a safe, magical little bubble. I could wait for hours, days, just to see that sweet, delicious smile and feel the hit as it entered my bloodstream. And then later, when she was gone, I would come down, sometimes slowly, sometimes sudden, and feel reality again, but not completely, still with an aftertaste of happiness that would flare every time I thought of her.

Yeah, yeah, Andy would say, big deal. It's impossible to explain. But it *is* a big deal, the biggest deal around.

♪ ♪ ♪

I took the jug back into the kitchen for more juice and there she was, with Lissa, laughing.

'Sounds like fun in here.'

I didn't hear what Cara said in reply. I was looking at her hair. She had whirled it around and stuck it up with something that looked like a short dark chopstick. When she turned you could see the smooth white nape of her neck, like a secret revealed.

'Can I help?'

Lissa told me to get together the cheeseboard and I told her to go outside and relax. She half-raised an eyebrow at me, but went. I felt fine. In fact, if anything, it was Cara who was nervous. I noticed her quietly destroying the sandwiches, so I said something – I don't know what, can't remember now. Anyway she threw one of them at me. I threw one back and then we were all right again.

She asked me about the tour.

'I hated it.'

'Food that bad?'

'Yeah, your pies lasted about an hour. Next time you really do have to come with us.'

I stole a glance at her beautiful neck and felt again that quivering lightness, that low, constant excitement humming through me. We were laughing together when Pam Frewen walked in and we both stopped and looked at her.

'Don't let me interrupt,' she said. 'Just came for some tonic.'

She took a bottle from the fridge and went out again, with chastened shoulders.

We were never alone for long. There were always people around that weekend. We couldn't get away from insipid people, babies and dogs. Even Pete annoyed me.

'Come on, Ade,' he said later that afternoon. 'Let's get the barbecue on.'

'Why is it always men who have to do the bloody barbecuing?' I asked. 'There's plenty of decent female cooks in the house.'

I looked towards Cara, lying in the hammock with a martini perfectly balanced on her flat stomach.

'We're on holiday,' said Lissa. 'Now shoo.'

Nick Frewen wandered over with us and handed me a beer.

'So, you're not married, Adrian?' he asked.

Pete spluttered.

'Adrian?' he said. 'You obviously don't know Adrian.'

Bloody Pete. He really was being annoying that afternoon. I figured Lissa must have told him something.

'I guess I just haven't met the right woman,' I said, as dignified as possible.

'Go on,' said Pete, tossing a steak like it was roadkill. 'You wouldn't get married even if you had.'

Nick rolled back on his feet and turned his head to inspect me.

'Would you?' he asked.

'I might.'

I hated feeling defensive. I swallowed more beer. Fuck it. Self-satisfied shits.

'Then again, I might not. I mean why the hell would you, if you didn't have to?'

'See,' Pete waved a beer bottle in my direction. 'Hardened bachelor. And good luck to him. Sorry we didn't invite any single girls for you, Ade.'

'Perhaps I'll try my luck with the married ones,' I said and walked back over to the women on the deck.

'Go away,' said Liss.

'Why? What are you girls talking about?'

'Our husbands,' said Pam.

'Carry on,' I said. 'I won't tell. Just think of me as an honorary woman for the afternoon.'

Cara giggled. It was easy for me to charm her. Especially when Michael was out of the way. Poor Michael. But why do I think that, when it was he who was the fortunate one, the one with the winning hand? It must be Cara's feelings rubbing off on me. She talked of him so admiringly. It was almost pathetic. The man sounded like an egg. For someone dealing with emotions, he sounded very detached, as if he hadn't felt a real emotion in the whole of his life. He was a bad influence on Cara, I'm sure of it. It wasn't that *she* wouldn't let herself feel. It's that *he* wouldn't let her.

Fuckin' shrink. I've never met a shrink who didn't ask more questions than was good for them. Not that I've met many shrinks. I've come across the odd one. Odd being the operative word. That's why they get into it, I reckon. They're all secretly mad as maggots. Questions, questions, questions. They never just talk to you like real people.

I can't understand people who live only in their heads like that. It's not healthy. I've always been a very physical person. If I'm feeling something too much, I have to do something physical. If I get really angry or sad or something, I work out, or play drums, or go for a walk in the rain. Maybe that's why I did the fire thing that night. I was showing off – and I was a bit drunk. But I was being me. It was the only me thing I did that whole weekend, and I didn't care what any of them thought. Well, just one of them. And she liked it. Or she said she did.

I always liked playing with fire, literally. Mum used to freak. But if you play right, if you're taught how to handle it, fire isn't dangerous, not if you're not afraid. It's beautiful, it's the most beautiful thing. I love listening to fire, really listening to it. The sound it makes when it ignites – the whoosh of life, of creation. And the sound as it burns, the devouring, the destruction. I like the risk.

I'm sure Mikey would have a field-day with that one, but he can go to hell.

It wasn't a premeditated thing, even if I was showing off. I just saw the long stick that Lissa had brought up from the beach leaning against the barbecue. It was perfect. Meths-soaked cloths on either end and we're away. I just did the basic routine. It's like juggling two balls of light, you twist and turn and whirl the stick faster and faster until they blur into one large circle of moving light, until all you can see is this huge fire snake chasing its own tail and all you can hear is the crackle of its tongue whipping around your skin. In the end I wasn't doing it for her, I wasn't even doing it for me – I was doing it for that snake. When I was there, in the middle of that circle of light and heat, the giant snake rose up on the tip of its tail and looked me straight in the eye. Its forked tongue snapped at my face and I heard it hiss, taunting me. I could see my own fear reflected back in its shining eyes as it pulled back its head to strike.

♪ ♪ ♪

Sol

IT'S HARD to know where that line between being in love and being obsessed starts and ends. I thought about her all the time. I imagined numerous different scenarios over and over. She would leave Michael, I would seduce her, we would go overseas to an exotic island. I followed her around sometimes. But I didn't see it as obsession. I was in love, and when you're in love these are the things you do. It wasn't until later that I realised some of the things could be seen as a little weird.

There was that time I was invited to her house for dinner. I arrived late. It wasn't until I was in, sitting amid purple cushions on a plush sofa, accepting a canapé and not allowing myself to look at her perfect panty-hosed legs, that I realised it was a proper dinner party. There were two other couples and a single woman – a buxom nurse named Sally, tanned, freckly and cheerful, with a laugh like a donkey – presumably meant to be teamed up with yours truly. I got bored with Sally and her braying after two minutes and couldn't help misbehaving. At least I waited until the second drink.

'So Neil, it is Neil, isn't it?'

'Neville.'

'How's business, Neil?'

'Neville. Can't complain. We're doing all right, considering the downturn. It's going to stay flat for a while yet, I'd say. It's this bloody government, raising taxes and compliance costs, they're going to drive the best businesses overseas soon. I'd go myself if it wasn't for Sharon here.'

'I thought you said you couldn't complain.'

'Ah. Yes.' He uttered a short, sharp bark of a laugh.

'Canapé, Neville?'

'Thanks, Car. Bloody gorgeous.'

'Why don't you tell Neville what line of work you're in, Adrian.'

'You a businessman yourself then?' He turned to me eagerly, a glitter in the sick yellow white of his eye. His teeth clicked together when he talked, as if they were false.

Cara always liked the game. She'd tell me off a little afterwards, in that sweet, low voice which couldn't ever tell anyone off. But she couldn't help laughing, and sometimes she'd even join in, so the public conversations became secret codes, obscure to anyone but ourselves, and each taunting pun a delicious, shared sin that thrilled more than a touch on the cheek or the brushing of legs under a table.

'Yes, Nigel. I'm a purveyor of euphonious reverberations.'

'Ah. Much in that then?'

'We're managing to drum up some interest.'

Her lips twitched.

I managed to speak to Cara alone only once, as I offered to help her clear the table.

'Shall I do the dishes?'

'No, no.' She was putting the coffee on. 'You go back out there and be rude some more. I don't think anyone's really taken offence yet.'

'You haven't, have you?'

'It would take a fair bit for you to offend me.'

'What would it take, I wonder?'

I wanted to grab her round the waist and kiss her, taste the pink smoothness of her mouth, but Michael's coffee machine started hissing.

'Where is Michael anyway?'

'He got called away to one of his suicidal clients. I wish they wouldn't choose to jump off bridges during our bloody dinner parties.'

'How inconvenient.'

'Here, take that tray in.'

'Don't send me back out there, not to mad Sally.'

'She's not mad.'

'She is. She neighs like a horse every time I say anything.'

Cara laughed. 'Don't be mean.'

'Are you trying to set us up? Because she is certainly under that impression. She keeps touching me.'

'Touching you?' Cara turned round from the machine, rather startled.

'My arm, my elbows, my hands. She's working her way down to my dick, I'm sure of it.'

'Adrian.' She turned back to the coffee. 'Tray.'

I sighed and went back into the lounge, trying to keep my distance from Sally. Unfortunately the only other spare seat was beside Neville. I loitered by it, inspecting a fine print on the wall.

'Sit down, Adrian. Tell us something about yourself.'

I suddenly realised I was drunk.

'I need to pee.'

'Down the corridor, third on the left,' said Cara.

I stumbled out of the room but forgot the instructions, opening a linen cupboard and then a door into a bedroom. Her bedroom. I went in quickly and closed the door behind me. I looked around, confused. I still needed to pee. Luckily there was an en suite so I went in and relieved myself, swaying a little, looking round the tiny white-tiled bathroom. It smelt of her. Ylang-ylang. I put a hand against the wall and closed my eyes, breathed it in. Why did I feel so sad at that? I came to before my head touched the wall, and zipped up, washed my hands. As I dried them on a bath towel, I saw a yellow linen laundry bag hanging from a hook on the door. It seemed perfectly natural to look through it. I found a pair of apricot under-pants and held them to my face and smelled. Her smell. A sweet, tangy smell, soft as spring grass. I put them back.

58

The bedroom was butter yellow with deep blue velvet curtains and a blue and white bedspread. Depressingly cheery. I tried not to look at the bed, to think . . . anything. I foolishly began to tiptoe across the polished wooden floorboards but stopped at a dressing table. There were a couple of photos in frames. One black and white picture was of a beautiful woman in her twenties; her long hippy hair suggested the 1960s, and she was carrying a baby. She looked a bit like Cara: the same thick, chestnut hair, the high cheekbones. It must have been her mum. So maybe the baby was Cara. How bizarre. To think of her as being a baby, somebody's daughter. The second photo was a colour shot of Cara and Michael on a small boat. He was in the forefront, holding some kind of a fish, and Cara sat behind, in shorts and a tee-shirt, with her rare smile, her long slim legs stretched out lazily in the sun. Somebody's wife. Then I spotted another photo pushed back on the dresser, edged behind the mirror. It was a close-up of a younger Cara. She must have been about 21, dressed up for a ball or something, in a pale blue silk dress, off the shoulder, her hair twisted elegantly and pinned up, a lone strand fallen in front of her ear. She was looking off to one side, not smiling but not sad, just caught in a moment of repose. Some people look ugly when you catch them like that. You see their anger in the set of their mouth, or their tired despair around their eyes. Cara simply looked calm, as if she was waiting for something good to happen, or for someone she loved.

I looked at the photo for what seemed like a long time.

She was younger but still the same Cara. I felt puzzled by it. It was impossible for me to imagine her living a life before I met her, as a joyful child, an anguished adolescent, a young, hopeful woman. It seemed as if she must have spent that life waiting, like in the photo, waiting for someone, maybe waiting for me. I heard the sound of a door closing out in the hallway and slipped the photo into my trouser pocket.

I don't know why I did that. Stupid. But it's not as if I took it home and worshipped it or anything. I didn't set it up on my bedside table and gaze at it adoringly every night or anything like that. In fact, I forgot I'd taken it. I was drunk. I don't even remember how I got home. I came across the photo a few days later when I was putting the trousers in the wash. Something clunked against the side of the washing machine so I pulled the trousers back out and searched the pockets. I was shocked to find the silver-framed photo, and for a moment I had no idea how it got there. Then I remembered. I thought about sneaking it back somehow, but it was impossible. So I just put it away. In one of those shoeboxes I keep in the wardrobe, full of old stuff I don't know what to do with. And I just forgot about it again. Honestly.

♪ ♪ ♪

I didn't see Cara for a while after that. I didn't even try. I didn't ring her work or her house. I think the photo thing might have freaked me out a little. I spent lots of time drumming instead, waiting for the composing to come. It didn't. And not seeing her didn't work. It didn't stop me thinking about her, wondering what she was doing. I couldn't help myself. Like I said, it was like an addiction. I even started imagining things. For a while I wondered if I was going mental. That line: I got pretty close to it.

One night in winter I came out of rehearsal around dusk and headed to a store to pick up a Nicolai Medtner CD I'd ordered. I was crossing the street when I saw a woman walk past. She was wearing a long purple coat and a fuchsia-coloured hat. I was sure it was Cara. I turned and automatically followed her, about half a block behind. She was walking quickly, with that little half-step that Cara does when she's in a hurry. She was wearing the same knee-high black boots she had on last time we went to a concert. She turned a corner at the library and I hurried to catch up. When I turned into the square there was no sign of her and I felt a strange panic as if I had lost something I'd been told to keep safe. Then a purple coat flapped from behind a sculpture and the black boots strode out across the square and I almost cheered. I tried to walk nonchalantly, as if I was just passing by, but she wasn't looking my way so I stepped up the pace a bit. She looked like she'd had a haircut, or maybe it was tucked up under her hat. I wondered where she was going. Maybe she was meeting someone for a drink. Once I caught up to her, I could find out where and say I was meeting someone there too. No, too obvious. I could just suggest we have a drink or a coffee. Or maybe she'd like to catch a movie. We'd gone to the movies together once.

I have no idea now what it was we saw. I can only remember it was funny, because she laughed, her lovely musical laugh that could carry clear across a room. And I'd laughed too, although I wasn't paying much attention to the screen. I just sat there, feeling grateful for simply sitting next to her, with her sleeve against mine and, once, the thrilling warmth of her breath on my face as she leaned over to whisper something about the story.

The purple coat stopped at a pedestrian crossing and I turned away and looked in a shop window. My face looked back at me in reflection. I looked happy. I don't know why; I wasn't smiling. I just looked happy.

I followed her across the road and up another block before she paused again, this time in front of a bus stop. She consulted the timetable and looked back up the road. I instinctively turned my head as well. A bus roared past me and stopped in front of Cara, and some people shuffled up to the door, obscuring her from my view. I started to run.

I got to the bus just as the doors were closing and, without thinking, I hammered on the glass. The driver turned his head and glared at me, hitting a button for the doors to slide open with a hiss that could have come from the man himself. He stared at me in challenge and grunted.

'Where to?'

I had no idea where the bus was heading, so I asked for two sections, hoping that would be long enough.

'Two-eighty.'

I handed him a crushed note and took the change

while looking down the bus for Cara. She was down the back, taking off her hat. I stumbled down the aisle as the bus lurched from the kerb and I swung from pole to pole, towards Cara. What would I say? Where could she be going? The fuchsia hat came off and I smiled at her, two poles away. She looked at me and looked away, out the window, the way you do when you accidentally meet the eye of a stranger who looks too long. It wasn't her. She had dark brown hair, but it was shorter; her eyes were blue, not brown. Her face a fraction wider, her eyebrows thicker. It wasn't her.

I stood for a while, not believing it, then sat down. I stayed on the bus for a few stops and got out just before the tunnel out towards the airport. I had to walk all the way back into town. It was then I decided I was going to stop. Stop trying not to imagine and then imagining. From then on I was going to go full out and find out what this thing was that had hold of me. Find out how far I could take it. It wasn't about sex. I didn't want to just have an affair. I was going to get Cara to fall in love with me.

♪ ♪ ♪

La

AND SO I started the plan. I worked it all out. I thought I knew just how to do it – Cara needed to find her rhythm, and then she would fall in love as naturally as a golden autumn leaf drifting gently from a tree. And so I set about providing the perfect conditions.

The background was music. We started going to concerts regularly, at least once a month, usually on a Friday. Not just the symphony orchestra, although Cara liked going to their concerts most. Sometimes I took her to the opera, or to a jazz club, or a seedy rock venue. Other people came occasionally, but usually we were alone. And it worked. I could feel her loosening up. It was in the way she held herself, the set of her shoulders, the greater frequency of that precious smile. I could hear it in her words.

'What do you feel like listening to tonight?' I asked her one Friday when there were three different concerts on.

'Whatever you would like, I would like,' she said.

'How full of trust you are.'

'No, not trust. Faith. You said once you needed faith and so I'm giving you some.'

I was so happy. Mostly. Sometimes I wondered what I thought I was doing. Why do we do the things we do? Does anyone really know what they're doing, let alone why? Most people just coast along most of the time, and life kind of happens. We're all in the driver's seat, though, making a left turn here, stepping on the gas, ripping along the motorway, stopping to find a map, but really, for some people, it's just kind of happening by itself for the most part. It's just habit. Like, they always go that way because they always go that way. It's like those journeys you take most often, where you know where you're going and you know how to get there and you've done it a million times before, like when you're driving to work, and you're thinking about something else entirely, so when you get there and get out, you actually have no memory of the journey and no idea how you got there at all. I suspect that's what life is like for a lot of people. Like my parents. They'll get to the end soon and have no idea how they got there because they were thinking about something else.

That scares the hell out of me. I'm determined not to let that happen. I mean, what a waste of time. What a waste of energy. I want to know exactly where I'm going. Even if you're not going to do anything with your life, you should at least notice what's happening. I'm amazed at the number of people who don't know what the hell is going on, and there's even more who think something else is happening entirely. I want to be one of those people who notice things – things other people take for granted or pretend aren't there because they don't understand them. I want to be one of those people on whom nothing is lost.

I thought at first that Michael didn't notice. That he was one of those 'blind' husbands. He wasn't. He made that clear to me on Cara's birthday. I still haven't worked out whether my respect for him went up, or down.

It was a mistake to send the flowers. They were too big, too bright, too bold. But I wanted to show her: see, this is what bold is.

It was another mistake to ring her. I should just have waited for that night. She'd invited me to join some friends at drinks and dinner. I could have waited until then.

But I didn't. I rang and when it answered, I launched into a rock rendition of 'Happy Birthday'.

'I presume you're wanting Cara,' said Michael.

'Oh. Yeah.'

'Can I say who's calling?'

'It's Adrian.'

'Ah. The man who takes my wife dancing.'

Oh great, great.

'Is she there?' I asked.

'Tell me,' he said. 'How do you think she is?'

'Who?'

'Cara. You've been seeing her a lot lately. How do you think she is?'

'Why?'

'I'm just trying to figure out something.'

'She seems fine to me.'

I wished he would put Cara on, but he persisted.

'Do you think she's happy?'

I guess I made the mistake of considering the question.

Was Cara happy? I don't think she was unhappy. That wasn't why – why me, I mean. She was trying to find something.

'She's happy if she doesn't think about it.'

'What do you mean?' I imagined Michael leaning towards me curiously.

'People can think too much. Thinking about whether you're happy is the quickest way to become unhappy.'

'You think she's unhappy.'

'I think she's thinking about it. Look, is she there or not?'

'I suppose it comes from being a psychotherapist,' Michael continued. 'But I tend to think that considering your state of being is quite a healthy thing. Do you not think about your feelings, Adrian?'

That's *so* Michael. He can't resist psychoanalysing everyone. I could tell even then he had his opinions about everyone all sorted out, no matter what you said to him. I knew there wasn't much point. But at the time I thought it was safer to talk about me than Cara. Now I think we were talking about her anyway.

'Like I said, you can think too much. It can stop you feeling. And if you stop feeling, what's the point in thinking?'

I heard a soft noise, almost a sigh.

'Go on.'

Go on. Like a fuckin' schoolmaster. Dig yourself deeper, son, so I can amuse myself in pointing out how you can no longer get out. Not without help. My help.

Still, I couldn't resist.

'Like when you're drumming. You're not thinking at all. It's just sensation. It's all feeling. In fact, if you start to think, it all gets fucked up.'

'So, the intellect fucks us up. Interesting.'

Obviously his analysis of me was in progress. I attempted a diversion.

'What about you, Michael? Are you happy?'

He stifled a mocking laugh.

'I haven't really thought about it.'

Smart-arse.

'So is Cara there?'

He finally got straight down to it.

'Lissa tells me you have a habit of making love to other people's wives.'

'Does she?' I would kill her.

'Is she correct?'

'No. It's hardly a habit. There may have been one or two examples.'

'Why do you think she told me that? I've been wondering if perhaps she thinks you're trying to seduce my wife.'

'I didn't think psychiatrists were so direct.'

'I'm a psychotherapist. There's a world of difference. Besides, that wasn't direct. I said "perhaps she thinks" not

"I believe".'

'Ah.'

I realised I was almost crouching down, holding the receiver with both hands.

'Psychotherapists also tend to read as much into non-replies as replies,' he said.

I was angry at the way I could feel my face reddening. I imagined him wearing a cocky smirk. I straightened up.

'Why should I bother then? You can have a nice little conversation all on your own.'

'I see. A neither confirm nor deny policy.'

I said nothing.

'You needn't worry. I'm not going to threaten you,' he continued.

I sputtered. The man was a joke. A malevolent little joke.

'As I say, this isn't a threat, or a warning, or anything of that nature. There's no need for that. Cara is completely free to do as she wishes. It's just a statement. I'm simply letting you know that I know.'

I sensed a small fear hiding behind his words.

'You know a lot, don't you, Michael?'

'I know one thing,' he said. 'I know how this will end.'

I almost laughed.

'In tears? Yeah, I saw that movie too.'

♪ ♪ ♪

Cara was turning thirty-five. She must have invited everyone she knew that night. When I got to the pub I was surprised to see about 50 people in her group, spread across a number of tables. I wasn't sure which one was Michael. I wanted to avoid him after that phone conversation. I went and talked to Pete and his brother Mark. I didn't get much of a chance to say hello to Cara properly, but she was everywhere I looked, greeting people, accepting a drink, gesturing with her hands in that dainty way she had when she was telling a story. She was very striking that night and hard to miss in her bright red skirt and shoes, with a black low-cut top and black lacy stockings. I dreamt about those stockings later.

Despite all her apparent spontaneity, Cara cared about image. I wonder now if that was all I was, part of the image. Not for anyone else's viewing, but her own private image that she tucked away in a pocket somewhere and took out every now and again to convince herself that her life was actually all right. I'm not bitter, I'm just trying to understand.

I stood with Pete and Mark, listening vaguely to them talk of sport, but I couldn't help watching Cara. I didn't care who saw. She looked different that night, with the group's focus on her. It lit her up somehow. It was as if she was *aglow*. It puzzled me and I watched her all that evening, trying to figure it out. I stared at the curve of her back, her hand touching her hair, wishing it was my hand. I liked watching her in public; it felt more permissible than when we were alone together. We were both free to be those public selves. In private, it was rather more frightening. Like me, I think Cara was afraid that her real self would not be so attractive. Alone, we circled each other warily, our conversation gently reaching out then turning to scurry away again. I don't know if she felt this way, but I'm sure she must have understood something of the secret underlying.

At one point, someone said something that made her lift her head and her hair fell back from her face, revealing wide brown eyes, a hint of a smile. Lissa took a photo just at that moment and the flash made me jump, the shock of brightness lighting up the memory in my mind like a flare exposing a small boat on a dark sea. For that moment she looked exactly like she did in the photo I had stolen. She had the same aura. Now I come to think about it, it was the same in all the photos I ever saw of Cara. She was what you call 'photogenic'. It's funny how some people look really great in photos. They look fine in person, but in photos they somehow stand out more: they have great teeth, perfect skin, they have that aura. Why does the camera do that to some people?

Other people noticed it too. 'Doesn't Cara take a great photo?' Pete said a few days later, as we looked through the party snaps.

'You wouldn't recognise her!' said Lissa.

'Yes, you would,' I said.

And I would. Because to me, Cara had that special-ness, that aura most of the time. It was as if I saw her through the same lens.

♪ ♪ ♪

Si

I FELT it immediately when I woke up that morning. My pulse was racing. Must've been dreaming – and I knew what about. I had big plans for that night. I got up, showered, had breakfast. My pulse was still fast. I lay two fingers on my wrist and counted, timing by the minute hand on my watch:125. Way too fast. The phone rang. It was JJ, he was waiting outside – I'd arranged for him to give me a lift to the rehearsal. I grabbed my gear and ran out to the car in the rain.

It was pissing down. We drove into town with the wipers on full bore, wheesh, wheesh, wheesh, wheesh. The radio was up loud and JJ was yelling above it. He was still spitting about the recording company guy from the other day. He kept saying, 'Who the fuck does he think he is?' The guy had been a real prick. We were offering to make him money after all. He just wanted to put us down. 'Power-fuckin-tripper,' said JJ.

I started to get shitty too. First about the recording guy and then 'cause JJ was so pissed off. The traffic was foul and it fucked him off even more. The mood in the car was totally claustrophobic. JJ was yelling at the bastards in front who wouldn't run the yellows, and the radio was screaming some Top 10 crap reeking of drum machines. Drum machines have a lot to answer for. It's rhythmic pollution. Drummers just don't play like that, with absolutely no variation. It's not real. It's got no *soul*. The stuff just drives faster and faster. It's no wonder every-one's always fuckin' rushing all over the place.

I could feel myself going under. I turned off the radio and told JJ to cool it.

I looked out the fogged-up window and wondered if Cara would come that night. She had to come. I had it all planned: that night would be the night. I listened to the sound of the rain and the wheesh-wheesh-wheesh of the wipers.

That was the day I composed my most famous piece, *Pulse*, the one that became so well known. I didn't call it that after the group, although I know they always thought I did. I called it that because my pulse wouldn't stop racing that day. I kept taking it every so often, and it was never below one hundred. I'm sure that's why the tempo of the piece is so fast. Toscanini was once con-gratulated after a performance of Beethoven's Ninth by a man who said he'd heard him conduct the same work 30 years earlier and the performance was identical.

74

Toscanini told him it wasn't – his pulse rate had been different that time. See, a pulse is constantly changing. Every little alteration in physiology, psychology, changes it. You can feel it. You can feel it in music too. The pulse of the music is its life force.

That afternoon I was sitting in the studio after the others had all left. I was fiddling around with the sound, multiplying tracks and speakers, until it went quadraphonic. As I sat there in the middle of the room, listening to the music on eight speakers, I realised it sounded different from the amalgamation of music you hear in a concert chamber. I tried to locate the sounds in space. There, the clarinet seemed to occupy the space upstage around the music stand. The trumpet was over by the bell tree, and the piano sound downstage, hovering around the double-headed Djun-djun. I closed my eyes and listened, really listened. It didn't correspond to the seating of the group during the recording; it was more like in the shape of something. I listened again. The sound areas were related like the head, arms and legs of a sculpture might be related. The music was drawing a visual picture.

That's when I got the idea. I switched off the music and found a pencil and some sheets. I closed my eyes and there, as always, she was. And I had faith. So I started to compose.

♩ ♩ ♩

That night I was filling in for a mate at his usual Salsa Club gig. It was perfect. I had it all planned. But when

I'd asked Cara, she hadn't been sure she could make it.

Michael, I thought. Bloody Michael.

We were into the third number when I saw her. She was standing with two other women near the door, watching. These things always start with a lesson for the newcomers: two expert dancers, Eduardo and Maria, stood in the middle of a circle of learners, patiently showing them step by step, over and over again. I kept playing the beat, watching Cara until I caught her eye. She smiled and quickly covered her mouth, gave a little wave. She looked a bit embarrassed. The next song, she and her two friends joined on to a line of learners and I couldn't see her so well. The place was packed.

I felt strangely relaxed, enjoying the music. The 'orchestra' was big, but it was informal, everyone doing their thing – singers, trombones, trumpets, bongos, congas, maracas. It was good for a bit of a laugh. Most of the players were strictly amateur, but enthusiastic, and not bad. I always enjoy playing with those who play just for the love of it. I like watching them concentrate on keeping time – now and then you see someone lose it. I like guiding them back home.

But I kept my eyes on the dance floor that night. Tangos, salsas, marimba. They were grooving. I relaxed and played and watched. Cara wasn't bad at the salsa – still learning obviously – but she'd got the steps and was starting to get a swing in her hips. She had nice round hips. You could tell it would be nice to put your arm around the small of her back, to bring those hips in to rest against yours, to lead her where you wanted to go. That's the thing about those dances – the roles for men and women are very distinct. I remember Cara saying later she liked that. 'It means you can relax more,' she said.

She was wearing a flared, dark blue skirt with a white strip along the bottom, and when she turned the white strip would swing and flap and turn back a split second after she had, like foam sucked back by a tide. Her black high heels stepped out delicately, turned and picked up pace with a little double-step of excitement. She had nice ankles – smooth white curves. As I watched her feet, I realised why men used to find ankles so attractive. She danced with a series of men, holding their hands, their waists. Her arms were held high, elbows bent. Her skirt turned and flared, her feet stamped and her eyes smiled, although her mouth was set in concentration. I think it was the most fun I'd ever seen her have.

During the break I grabbed a couple of beers and went up to Cara just as she was coming up to me.

'You look like you've done this before.'

'Only once.'

And she smiled at me, a wide, red grin that I just wanted to fall into.

'I've learnt to smile,' she said.

A few weeks before, I'd been showing her how to play a dombeq. She'd been concentrating too hard, a little wrinkle across her forehead, playing correctly but too perfectly. I'd stopped her. 'You're playing everything right, but you're doing it wrong,' I said. 'You're not smiling.'

Now here she was, smiling away. I could hardly speak. I held up my bottle.

'Here's to you.'

We clinked. Her friends came up and she introduced them: Tracey and Louise. Louise was very chatty. She'd heard of Pulse and wanted to know when we were next performing. I talked without really noticing her, all the time my eyes on Cara, watching her sip her beer, adjust her shoe strap, rest a hand lightly on her hip. Her ring glittered at me. The band started regrouping and one of them waved to me. Tracey and Louise ran off to the loo.

'You better go,' said Cara.

'Yes.'

I didn't move.

'Would you like to dance?' she said.

She put her beer down on a nearby table and came up to me, took my arm.

I didn't move. The band was already starting up.

'Like you said, I better go.'

'They'll survive without you for one song.'

She tugged a little on my arm. 'Come on. You're not smiling.'

And so we danced. It was a marimba. Fast. I got confused. Right foot forward, right foot back, one two, one two, left forwards, left back. We stumbled and she laughed.

'Let me lead.'

So I stopped trying to pretend I knew what I was doing, and let her take over. Her hand firm in mine, her eyes on mine. And one two, one two, there we were, doing it, dancing, moving in time to the music. All I could hear was my heartbeat, all I could see were her eyes, all I could feel was the shape of her body against mine, the softness of her breath on my neck. I could hardly look at her, couldn't not look. It was like I didn't know her any more. She'd found it.

♪ ♪ ♪

Red

LOVE. WHAT is love anyway? At the end of it all, that's the question I keep coming back to. I have a lot of questions still. But mostly they're just detail, minor detail, and in the end I have to keep returning to the bigger picture. I feel that if I could answer that main question, that single question that so many have pondered down the ages, then none of those other things would matter. But I can't. I don't know anyone who could.

Adrian could answer most of the smaller questions, if he chose to. But they don't really figure and I can't ask him now anyway. I can't ask Cara either – she won't talk about it any more. She thinks I see this as a case study. I don't. Well, I try not to. It's a bit too personal for that.

It's not that I don't understand what happened. I do. I'm not sure how any of us could have done much differently. For a while I thought it was my fault, but then I came to see it wasn't. It wasn't Cara's fault either. No one can choose who they fall in love with. Can they? I keep wondering whether Adrian manufactured it somehow.

'Falling' in love is, of course, different from love itself. Love is not just a passionate spark, it's a way of being. The 'falling', however, precipitates an exclusive love, feeding on itself, neither giving to nor caring about others. It is not, as some think, evidence of 'purity'. It is destined to cave in on itself.

I wouldn't say I fell in love with Cara immediately. There was no 'falling' involved. I think, rather, that I recognised who she was. I'm one of those people with very strong intuition. I didn't realise it was such a rare quality until I was well into my adult years.

When I met Cara, I intuitively knew there was something special about her – about us together. It may be presumptuous to use the phrase 'meant to be', but really, that is how I felt, despite the faintly pathetic circumstances of our first blind date. Neither of us was with anyone at the time and a mutual friend had given me Cara's number. We met for lunch at a coffee bar down-town. Lunch seemed like an easy option. Not that I thought so while I was sitting alone in the crowded café, waiting for Cara to turn up and realising that neither of us knew what the other looked like. I drank a whole jug of lemon water waiting, and when this woman came up to the table I stood up, meaning to go to the bathroom, but it turned out to be Cara. The first thing I thought, when I realised it was her, was that she was younger than I had expected. Then I thought she was more beautiful than I had expected. Then I suddenly thought: 'I'm going to marry this woman.'

It's that level of intuition that's made me the person I am. I'm sure it's that intense awareness of mood and emotion, in others as well as in myself, that led me into psychology. It's the connection with behaviour that fascinates me – why people behave the way they do. It's only when you find out the why that you have the chance to alter the what. If that's what you're after, of course. Some people find change too hard, but even without change, simply understanding things has got to be good for you. I have to believe that. Meanwhile, I'm still trying to understand myself, never mind Cara or Adrian.

The key to it all, I believe, is to love oneself. That's basically what I try to teach most of my clients, when it comes down to it – how to love themselves. It does help to understand oneself first, so that's where we start: why they are who they are. That one can take rather a while, and indeed, some never get it at all, they're so determined to evade themselves. Once that's achieved, though, self-love is usually a relatively simple matter. Once they understand what's going on, they can forgive – not always others, but often themselves.

Psychobabble, Adrian would call it. Maybe it is babble, but it helps. Helps some anyway. Those who choose to think about such things. That's where I have to admit to contempt for Adrian. It's not that I hate him. I've searched my feelings for him thoroughly. What I mainly find is a kind of curiosity. Why, why, why? That's how I interact with the world. I question. I seek meaning. That's what I still find hard to understand about Adrian. The man never questions his own feelings, let alone other people's feelings. Everything is the way he says it is and let's get on with it. Well, sometimes things aren't the way they seem – we've all learnt that.

I'm a firm advocate for the truth, in all its many and varied forms. Because, while the pain may be greater – though not in the long run – the rewards are so much more. The apprehension of truth is like seeing something beautiful for the first time: the brilliance of a colour or a light. It's like the dawning of a rainbow.

Cara gets annoyed when I say things like that. She's not what I would call a patient person. Although she's better than she used to be. When I first met her she was really raring to go. I guess that's one of the things I liked about her – all that energy, just looking for a focus. For a while I used to think it was me. She'd be the first to admit that when we met she was a bit, well, not 'awed', but impressed by me. I was older, more experienced. Not that I take too kindly to the father-figure theory. Maybe there was a touch of that to begin with, but not any more. The age gap is no longer relevant. And I'm sure it's coincidental that Adrian is younger. I come back to the question of why she fell into his trap. What was she looking for? Love? Ah. And what is love anyway?

But why would she look for love? Cara had love. I always loved her. She knew that. Perhaps it was lust. But it's not that simple. Lust may have been there, of course, maybe even in equal measure. But you cannot confuse the two – too many people have this problem. It is generally quite easy to distinguish them. You simply examine your private thoughts (again, a thing some have difficulty with) and note the times you think about sex, the other's body, your own, that sort of thing. Then you note the number of times you think about the other's person – their ideas, their thoughts, opinions, actions, behaviour, emotions and so on. Lust versus love. Remarkably easy really. It can get rather mixed up, I concede, but it's not that hard to see which will last. So, I'm ignoring the lust. That was always my conscious choice. I deliberately tried to disregard any possibility of lust.

But their love – now that was of interest to me. What lay behind Cara's love: that was the key. The key to keeping her. That was, of course, my motivation all along. I freely acknowledge it. I would be remarkably relaxed, after all, if I didn't have some interest in keeping the love of my wife. I suppose that was not necessarily in question. I daresay you can love two different people at the same time. But such different people! Regardless, I was determined not to give her up.

My resolve really formed the night I sat up waiting for her. She'd told me she was going to a movie. But what movie finishes at 3 a.m.? I sat up waiting, watching TV until it got too ghastly and I switched it off and went to bed with a book on phobias. I couldn't concentrate, kept checking the clock-radio by the side of the bed, each time its red numerals glaring at me only a few digits on from when I last looked. An accident, I thought. Maybe I should ring the hospital. I must've fallen asleep because I jerked suddenly at the sound of the garage door closing. My book was still in my hand. The clock said 3.40 a.m. I dumped the book on the floor and switched off the light so Cara would think I was asleep. It seemed an age before she tiptoed in. I tried to keep my breathing deep and regular.

'Michael?' she whispered.

I didn't reply. I heard her go into the bathroom and wash her face, brush her teeth, then a soft swishing by the side of the bed as she undressed and got in beside me. She snuggled up to my back and put a cold arm around me. I grunted.

'Sorry I'm so late,' she said. 'We went dancing.'

I remained silent. Soon her own breathing was deep and even and her arm relaxed and dropped from my waist. I lay there and thought, I need to know more about this. I need to find out what's going on.

That's when I started keeping watch. I watched for signs. And I started thinking about why. I'm still thinking about why. I'm convinced there must have been something in our relationship that *allowed* it to happen. But, it seems, the more I deliberately pursue meaning, the more it eludes me.

Why did Cara love him? She denies it now. But I'm convinced she did. I need to find out what it was that drew her to him. I don't think it was merely his manipulation, his web of deception. There was something in her that responded. Why? Why, when it came to that, does she love me? This is what I feel I have to focus on now. I feel a need to assume some responsibility for the problem. That comes from being a therapist, of course. But if we don't assume responsibility for how we help to create our problems, we cannot change. I think Cara and I need to change.

I'm doing a lot of reading on the subject of love. But it's all academic, until you apply it to particular circumstances. What is love? Love is a desire. A desire for what? Maybe a desire to possess. Did Cara desire to possess Adrian in some way? Possess some aspect of him, his air of confidence, his approach to life, his way of being? That's what I thought for some time, before I knew him properly. Now that prospect scares me.

Of course, there's always the opposite impulse: the desire to be possessed, or the desire to surrender. That way feeds admiration, adoration, the setting on a pedestal, the loss of any sense of responsibility. Oh, very seductive, I'm sure. But Cara? I really think Cara is too much of a control freak for that. A more muted abdication of responsibility perhaps – the desire to find again a father or a mother. Freud's big on this one, though I don't have a lot of time for him. He may have got it right occasionally, but it's obvious the man had problems of his own. Besides, the age thing makes me a more likely candidate for the father figure. Of course, it may be complicated by the fact that Cara had two fathers: Eddie – now there's an excellent example of refusal of responsibility – and her stepfather James. I think Cara was a lot more affected by James's death than she admitted, even to herself. But that wasn't until later. The other desire is simple. Deadly simple and the most effective of them all. The 'biological motive'. Babies.

So that's what I started with. A bunch of disparate desires, one or more of which may have been a factor in Cara's emotional make-up. But I wasn't convinced by any of them. I wanted to go deeper. I wanted to find out what was really going on.

♪ ♪ ♪

Orange

THE MORNING after Cara had stayed out so late, I was the first to raise the subject. I was trying not to make anything of it, but I see now it would have been better to just come right out and tell her how I felt. That's always what I advise. But it's not so easy when you don't feel entitled to feel what you're feeling. Instead, I just asked her a simple question.

'What time did you get in last night?'

She looked at me. 'I'm not sure.'

It would have been better just to leave it alone. But I couldn't help myself. It was the implied guilt.

'Must've been late. I didn't go to bed until around one.'

'Yeah.'

She reached forward, took an orange out of the fruit bowl and started peeling it slowly.

'We went clubbing.'

Not just dancing, 'clubbing'.

'I thought you were going to the movies.'

'After the movies.'

'After the movies you went "clubbing"?'

'Mm hm.'

I helped her finish clearing up. Neither of us said anything more. Not until that night anyway, when we were going to bed. Again, I couldn't help myself.

'You must be tired after your late night.'

'No. I enjoyed it. I might go again next week.'

'I didn't know you liked dancing.'

'Well, I do.'

'Maybe I should try it some time.'

'I don't think you'd like it, Michael.'

'Are you angry at me?'

'For God's sake.'

I went into the bathroom for a while. It always helps to have a short break, to think. When I got back she was in bed, with her light off. I got into my side and picked up a book. Her voice was soft.

'Come if you want, Michael. You know you won't like it.'

'I probably wouldn't. That's okay, you go. I just want you to be happy.'

Silence.

I wasn't trying to make her feel guilty. I was trying to let her have some space, to do the things she needed to do. I was. I know the right things to say, and I said them. Sometimes too late maybe, sometimes without the appropriate sentiment, but nobody's perfect.

Neither of us is good at conflict. I've certainly improved in that area. And I'm sure conflict can be positive; I've seen it become a learning experience for my clients often enough. If we can better understand what we're saying and why, I'm sure it helps. Cara says I over-analyse, but she's no better on the spot than I am. It's hard at the time, when you're caught up in the heat of the moment. I hate that. I usually have to take the thing away and think about it.

Of course, you don't always have that luxury, as I discovered.

Communication is the key. It's not just about talking, saying how you feel and so on. It's about listening, active listening, so everyone understands each other. You can talk all day and still someone can completely miss the point. People don't pay enough attention to words. They make assumptions, jump to conclusions, interpret others by using the wrong references. A literal person talking to an intuitive person doesn't have much hope. They just drive each other crazy.

I remember one couple I was counselling was always having this problem. She was completely literal and could never understand why her replies to simple questions used to drive her husband nuts. The classic example was when they were in a rush to catch a plane and were hurrying to return a rental car to the airport.

'What type of car is it?' he asked.

'A Ford,' she replied.

'Yes, but what type is it?'

'A Ford Telstar.'

She was just trying to be helpful. But of course he wanted to know which rental agency to return it to. They were always missing each other like this, until they worked out that they thought differently and started translating each other better. Partners don't necessarily have to speak the same language – but it helps.

The trouble is, opposites attract. A couple may be entranced with the differences at the beginning of the relationship, but as it wears on and the contrasts appear every day in practical things, the annoyances build up. And because each of them deals with conflict differently, the thing never gets sorted. I had one client couple who were like that. He was an introvert, she was an extrovert. They were attracted to each other because of that very difference. (According to the 'I need you to feel complete' school of thought.) So, while he was attracted to her confident conversations and she appreciated his listening, when it came to conflict it was a disaster. She would talk more loudly and quickly and he would become more quiet and withdrawn. ('Your silence drives me crazy. It's so controlling!' 'You never listen and your loudness is embarrassing.') Short cut to explosion.

They just didn't understand each other's differences. These two were both accusing the other of lying, when really they were just misunderstanding each other. In arguments, she tended to exaggerate to underscore a point. He heard the hyperbole and thought it a bare-faced lie. Meanwhile, he wasn't disclosing certain things and she saw this as deliberately trying to hide the truth.

Neither was really lying; they just needed to understand what the other was doing. He needed to speak up more, and she needed to listen. They got there eventually. With my help.

Mind you, conflict can be hard for any couple to deal with. Even the same type of people. Get two introverts together, for instance, and when in strife they both withdraw. I guess that's what Cara and I are like. Cara may have fooled Adrian into thinking she was an extrovert, but that was just playing for his attention. She's as introvert as they come. I should know – it takes one to know one. You can tell by the way she rehearses things. She's always self-editing. She holds entire conversations in her head. I only found this out when she started saying, 'But I told you that . . .' when she hadn't. Then I realised I do exactly the same thing. Except I pay more attention to filing my fantasies. The paradox is, self-awareness brings anxiety.

I take care not to point these things out directly. I may hint, but usually I let Cara figure things out for herself. I can't do it for her. It's the same with clients. You have to let them get there for themselves. Maybe that was part of the problem. Maybe Cara was becoming more independent and I wasn't ready to deal with it. I'll have to think about that.

It's just as well I have my supervisor Jeremy to talk to. Sometimes he feels more like my therapist. I go to him once a week and we discuss cases and my handling of them, then any personal issues I need to talk about. At first I concentrated mainly on the cases, but Jeremy encouraged me to talk about myself. He's the first of my supervisors to do so, and I discovered I really enjoyed it. It's good to experience what it's like on the other side of the fence, to see how difficult it is to talk about very personal issues, to be completely honest with someone. I've realised how rare that is, and how valuable. I wish now I'd told him everything from the beginning.

I did talk to Jeremy in a round-about way about Cara. At that point, I was still trying not to talk to Cara about Cara. I was afraid I would be too emotional, with too much of a vested interest to deal with her in the best way. I might have got angry. Still, that couldn't have been any worse than what did happen.

I got angry a few times in the sessions with Jeremy. He got me to recognise the anger. That was useful. And a valuable exercise professionally. It can be surprisingly hard to know that you're angry. It's even harder to get to the next step – recognising that behind the anger lies fear. And recognising fear is sometimes all you need to do to stop being afraid. When I think back to those early sessions, I can't believe how blinkered I was.

J: How are you and Cara getting on?

M: Good, really good. Well, we haven't been seeing a lot of each other lately; we've both been really busy.

J: Busy.

M: I've had this conference to prepare for, as you know. And Cara's been going out a lot. She seems to have made some new friends and she's started doing different things with them.

J: What kind of different things?

M: Oh, shows, concerts, that sort of thing. One of these friends is a musician, so she's been getting free tickets to concerts.

J: Do you go along?

M: No.

J: Why not?

M: Well, like I said, I've been busy. And I'm not really into that sort of music – percussion. It's too loud. I went to one of their shows and I didn't like it. It was just noise. I told Cara that and she hasn't asked me again.

J: Cara likes this music.

M: She seems to. I was surprised. I wouldn't have thought she'd be into it at all.

J: What does she like about it?

M: I asked her that. She just said the rhythm. I don't understand it.

(*Pause*)

J: You don't understand it.

M: The appeal, I mean. I don't understand the appeal. Banging on all those drums. It sounds to me like they're playing from an angry place, you know.

J: That's interesting.

M: What? You think I'm projecting? I'm not angry, believe me, I'd know if I was angry.

J: What do you have to be angry about?

M: No, that's not it. And I don't think Cara's angry either. She's just doing what I've always told her to do – explore life for herself. It's a good thing. I don't want either of us to be too dependent on each other. I've seen how unhealthy that is.

J: So you like Cara going out more?

M: Yes. Yes, I do. It's good for her. If I miss her sometimes that's just the price I pay.

J: You feel you're paying for it.

M: You know, Jeremy, I can see how clients sometimes get annoyed at our techniques. Statements and questions, statements and questions. It's really rather tedious at times. I think I might introduce a more varied format in my sessions. Perhaps I'll just ask the client to talk on for a while, uninterrupted. It's really valuable for me to experience this, to see what it's like from the other point of view. You just want your therapist to sit down and tell you how to fix everything. So I can see how annoying it would be for the therapist to insist you work it out for yourself. Quick fixes, that's what people want these days. That's what we expect. There's no way for us to cater for that, though, is there? If you're a psychiatrist, it's all very easy: diagnose and give them a pill for the problem. Psychoanalysts at least have the comfort of their convictions about the necessary technical procedures. Even if that is an illusion. Psychotherapy, though, it's just a blind groping towards what's really going on. There's no getting away from sitting down and talking, talking, talking, fronting up and answering the unanswerable questions.

J: What *is* really going on, Michael?

M: You know, I have no idea.

(*Bursts out laughing.*)

♪ ♪ ♪

Yellow

IF ONLY I hadn't arrived late that Saturday night at Melissa and Peter's beach house. I would have met Adrian in person then. By the morning he was gone, damn it. He must have been avoiding me deliberately. I wonder how far advanced his plans were by then.

When I finally arrived, Melissa was the only one up, feeding the baby. She looked tired.

'Sorry I'm so late,' I said. 'Work got in the way again.'

'That's okay. Sit down and have a drink.'

I made myself a whisky and sat on the couch opposite. It was hard not to watch her breastfeeding. The baby was almost asleep, sucking peacefully.

'It would have been better if you'd come earlier,' said Melissa.

'Why? Did Cara miss me?'

'No,' she said. 'That's the problem.'

'What do you mean?'

'Have you not noticed how friendly she's getting with Adrian?'

Even though she was simply echoing my own suspicions, it was a shock to have them confirmed. I swallowed hard.

'I trust Cara,' I said.

'Of course, darling. But I wouldn't trust Adrian, if I were you.'

'I thought he was one of your friends?'

'Well, he used to be. The more I see him, the more insincere he appears.'

'You don't think . . . are they?'

I had another gulp of whisky. I couldn't even voice it.

'No, I don't think they're having an affair yet. But I'd watch out. Something funny's going on.'

The baby's mouth slipped off her nipple, the tiny face blissful. It failed to comfort me.

♪ ♪ ♪

I opened the door to the attic room slowly, so as not to wake Cara. But she was propped up in bed, staring across the room, her hands folded across her stomach, completely still.

'Are you okay?' I asked.

She turned towards me with a start.

'Hi, hon. Can't sleep, that's all.'

'You probably had too much to drink.'

She giggled. 'Probably.'

'Would you like a massage?'

'Mmmmm.'

I got up on the bed and she rolled over. I put her head in my lap.

'Let me do your head.'

There's nothing like a scalp massage for relaxing. I like to imagine I'm draining away all the tension.

I began stroking Cara's face, massaging around the forehead and temples. Slow, smooth, secure, reassuring. I imagined pushing away her worries, lifting the anxiety. Quick strokes towards the back of the skull. Pushing, stroking, soothing. And then my fingers dug in deeper, driving paths through her soft brown hair. I pushed it back and pulled it forward, pushed it back, pulled it forward, pushed and pulled and smoothed and smoothed. My fingernails made a little crackling noise like reaping grass, like wind in leaves, like the ocean whispering to a beach. I stopped and held her head in my hands. Her breathing was slow and quiet. She'd fallen asleep. I kept holding her head for a while, wondering what was going on in there. Then I set her down gently and got up. Now it was me who couldn't sleep.

I went downstairs. All the lights were out. I stepped out the back door and headed down to the beach. The moon was just past full and its light cast everything into silver. Clouds scudded over quickly, throwing shadows. It was kind of strange, light and yet dark, the air warm. I walked down the sand to the sea. I stood there for a long while, my hands in my pockets, looking up at the yellow moon with its mysterious face, listening to the sound of the waves. Shush shhh, shush shhh, shush shhh. There was a study done once where investigators took the pattern of brain waves and translated it into sound. When people were asked what the sound was, they invariably said, 'The ocean.' Is that why the sound of the ocean is so therapeutic? The pulse of the ocean is just like that of the brain. The rhythm of life.

♪ ♪ ♪

I woke late the next morning. I reached my hand out across the sheets and felt absence. I opened my eyes and checked my watch: 10.10 a.m. I had a quick shower, then went out to the deck, where the others were sitting around the remnants of brunch. I couldn't see anyone who might be Adrian and I couldn't help asking.

'Hi guys. Am I the only one up late?'

'Adrian's just left,' said Melissa, smiling at me in a sympathetic fashion.

'That's a shame. I was looking forward to meeting him,' I said.

Did Cara blanch? She might have, but then again I might have been imagining it. Quite often I imagine people have the reactions I expect them to have. It's a habit I'm trying to train myself out of. Jeremy picked it up.

Pete introduced me again to Nick and Pamela Frewen, who I'd met before at several dinner parties. I didn't particularly like them. I don't think they even liked each other much. The way they interacted together struck me as odd. They never looked at each other. And they were always sniping.

'Of course, Pam would go to every film at the festival, if . . .'

'. . . Nick would let me.'

'Well, I don't want to sit through all those bleedin' love stories.'

'Why not? You might learn something. Besides, I sit through all your action crap.'

'You like action movies.'

'Yeah, that's what you always say. Perhaps you could actually ask me one day.'

'Don't you like action movies?'

'No.'

'First I've heard of it.'

If they were my clients, I wouldn't give them more than a 30 percent chance of staying together. They were always getting irritated at each other and then were annoyed at doing it in front of other people. I wondered if they behaved like that when they were alone, but somehow I didn't think so. You can never tell, of course. You can never tell what a relationship is like from the inside unless you're party to it. If they'd socialised separately, I'm sure they'd have been much happier. It's funny, but I can't recall having a conversation with either of them on their own. They always stuck together in social situations, and then resented each other for it.

Thank God Cara and I aren't like that. When we go out to a social engagement, we naturally split off and hold our own separate interactions, then afterwards we compare notes about who said what to whom. That way you get to experience two different versions of the same event and sample more people. That's my theory anyway. I have to admit it began as a way for me to encourage Cara to become more social. When we were first going out I liked to throw her in at the deep end a bit. Not that I wasn't supportive, but I tried to show her she didn't need me. Obviously, I was too bloody successful.

For the rest of that day, I watched Cara from a slight distance. She was certainly happy. She gives off a kind of radiance when she's happy. Mind you, I think I find her more beautiful when she's sad. I can always tell if she's sad just by looking in her eyes. They have a poignancy about them that is striking. Anyway, Cara that weekend was especially attractive, I thought. She was unusually outgoing, talking a lot. I felt . . . proud of her.

It seemed harder to believe Melissa's warning in the bright sun of day. We went for a walk on the beach together, and Cara held my arm and leaned her head on my shoulder. I vowed to myself to pay more attention, to ensure I gave more gestures of love. Why does the memory make me feel sad? I suppose it's because of the illusion we were still clinging to. The illusion we were safe.

That broke for me when we got back home that night. The phone rang. Cara was in the bath so I answered it.

'Hello?'

There was a small pause. I could hear someone breathing on the other end.

'Hello?'

A click. And suddenly it was real again.

Funnily enough, that wasn't the real clincher. That came when I went up to the bedroom. The bathroom door was ajar, and I could see in the mirror a reflection of Cara lying in a foam bath. Her hair was pulled up and her eyes were closed. Her face seemed very bare, open. She was lying there, smiling to herself. That's really what did it for me. I just knew.

I also knew I was going to have to do something about it. I wanted Cara to make her own decisions, I wanted her to explore whatever it was she needed to explore, but that didn't mean I was just going to sit back and let that little . . . I wanted to remind her of us and what that meant, to even the odds. I wanted to fight.

That was how I lost my anxiety. It somehow turned into a kind of excitement. Whenever I heard Cara or anyone mention Adrian, it was like I became super-alert. I could feel the adrenaline. It was like I was readying for a fight. It was a private mental fight.

Adrian would say that's my problem: I live in my head. I admit it. Of course I live in my head, we all live in our heads to some degree – our perception determines how we interpret events, down to the point of determining the very events themselves. If we believe something happened, it might as well have happened. Of course it was just denial, but back then I kept asking myself: what if all this was just in my head? What if Cara wasn't really in love with Adrian? What if he wasn't in love with her? What if it was just my jealous perception that placed that

interpretation on events? All evidence was circum-
stantial, after all. And I am inclined to invest things with
meaning. Being a therapist, I tend to over-analyse. As
Cara says, sometimes a banana is just a banana.

Whatever the truth, at least I wasn't worried by it any
more. I was excited. I lay in bed that night and I thought,
This is a chance for something. If I'd had the slightest
idea of what was really going to happen, I think I would
have given up then and there.

♪ ♪ ♪

Green

IT WAS around that time I started seeing Vincent as a client. He'd been referred by his GP, Tom Sayers, a friend of mine. Tom warned me about him a few weeks before he turned up.

'He's a new patient of mine and I don't know him very well. But it looks to me like he's got some kind of serious disorder,' he said.

'Is he depressed?'

'No, it's more sinister than that. I do think he should be on some kind of medication, but I'm not sure what.'

'So why didn't you refer him to a psychiatrist?'

'I did. He wouldn't go. Said he'd been to one before and the drugs just spaced him out. He said he would prefer a psychotherapist. He even suggested your name.'

'I'll see what I can do,' I said.

I didn't really approve of medication then. Too many people were doped up, taken out of the real world, in my view. Now I see I was wrong. Drugs obviously help bring some people back into reality.

But the first time I saw Vincent, I forgot what Tom had said about medication. I saw an ordinary young man in an ordinary suit with ordinary problems. Vincent strode in confidently and sat on one of the side chairs, looked me right in the eye. Ah, I thought, one of those. Some men, you can tell almost immediately, they never learned to connect. They always pull back in therapy. I find them hard work. I have to make myself resist echoing the disconnection. Anyway, Vincent and I had the usual opening discussion and I let him vent a few scornful comments before I tackled him.

'You don't really want to be here, do you?'

'No.'

'And yet you asked your GP to refer you here.'

'He seemed to think it would help.'

'But you don't?'

'No.'

'Why not?'

'I can't stand all these psychological theories,' he said. 'Freudian, Jungian, New Age. I don't want to be objectified.'

'I don't think anyone does,' I said.

'People think those labels help somehow. But they don't. How does it help to know you're obsessive or aggressive? You are what you are. But no one wants to be who they are any more. So they look to you guys for instant solutions. Who says you've got all the answers?'

'People don't necessarily want solutions,' I tried to explain. 'They want to talk. They're just looking for some recognition or reassurance. What's wrong with that?'

But he'd touched a nerve with me. I haven't got all the answers and I know it. I often feel uncertain in sessions, as if I'm groping my way along. When people treat me like the fount of all knowledge, I'm often left with a tinge of fear. How do I avoid getting in over my head? What makes me think I can help this person? What's the payoff for me?

'All this emphasis on definitions,' Vincent continued. 'We have to define all these emotions. What's with that?'

'Well, understanding emotions can help some people to express them.' I was starting to get annoyed and trying not to show it. 'If people can recognise their emotions at the time they're feeling them, they can express them better.'

'I'd rather stay detached and in control.'

'That makes intimacy much more difficult,' I said.

Vincent just looked at me, his eyes unblinking.

'So, what's your school of thought then? I want to know who I'm dealing with.'

'I don't think it would help to talk about my theoretical orientation. Talking about schools of therapy will simply take us further away from the personal discourse we need to explore.'

'You're not going to tell me anything about your approach?'

'I'll tell you my main credo: "the unexamined life is not worth living".'

He didn't look impressed. I tried to reassure him.

'You should know I always take a treatment contract very seriously,' I said. 'Once I accept someone for treatment, I commit myself to stand by that person, to spend the necessary time and energy, and to relate to that person in a genuine manner. And I expect the same in return. It's the relationship that heals.'

I really meant that at the time. It didn't quite work out that way.

It took me a while to work the conversation back on track. We started to talk about his life. Now that I think about it, I should have spotted it straight off: it was classic. Grew up without a father, neglected by his mother, alcoholic, didn't seem to last long in any town or any job. He was charming, though, very charming, a completely normal façade. I quite enjoyed talking to him. When it was nearing the end of the hour, I tried a provocative question.

'So, if you don't believe in psychology, why are you here?'

'My wife sent me,' he said.

'Ah. Perhaps I should be seeing your wife, do you think?'

There was something in the way his eyes flicked, just a minuscule movement, which indicated something more.

'Perhaps you should,' he said evenly.

'What do you think might be wrong with your wife?'

There was a pause of a minute or a minute and a half.

That's a long silence in therapy.

'I think she's having an affair.'

A breakthrough. Vincent put his head in his hands as if he was weeping. I thought for a moment he was, when suddenly he pulled himself up and scratched at his face, glared at me. At the risk of leaving it up in the air, I thought it a good moment to draw to a close.

'Perhaps we should leave it there for today. I can see you at the same time next week.'

He looked uncertain.

'I'm not sure I can come next week. I've important meetings to prepare for. I can't be unprepared. I don't want to lose respect.'

Obviously he didn't want to be seen as needing to come. He stood up and gathered his briefcase and coat.

'I don't know if I can come in next week,' he repeated. 'I'll call you.'

Fine, whatever, I wanted to say. But I thought, No, look beyond it, see the underlying need. First-time clients often need reassurance.

'Your pain is valid, Vincent, and we'll find a way to talk about it.'

He looked sceptical. He went towards the door.

'I really can't come next week.'

I made a last effort.

'I'll be here next week and it's important that you be here too. I hope you'll come.'

He left me feeling foolish, as though I'd failed to engage him.

The next week I wasn't really expecting him to turn

up, but when I opened the door to the waiting room there he was. He came in and shook my hand.

'The fact that you said you'd be here for me is the only reason I came,' he said and sat down.

And so we reached an understanding. At least, I thought we did.

It was during the third session that I first got a glimpse of the subterfuge going on. It wasn't just that I was gaining his trust; he was gaining mine. Oh, he was clever all right. By the end of the hour, I found myself in a most peculiar position: I was talking about myself to a client. Not in a general way, not in that non-specific way I sometimes might – this was direct.

'There's nothing definite, you know,' he said. 'No real, undeniable proof. That's the worst of it. If I knew for sure, then I'd be able to deal with it.'

It wasn't until much later that I discovered he was lying the entire time. But, of course, there I was, Mr Sympathetic. I got sucked in by one of the first lessons you learn: never answer their personal questions.

'She's so bloody secretive,' he said. 'Mind you, women are like that. Is your wife secretive?'

'I suppose she is, sometimes. Not secretive as such, but private. She keeps private things close to her.'

'Ah. And does she lie to you? But then, you wouldn't necessarily know if she lied to you, would you? That's the mind fuck.'

I didn't answer that one. It was the 'mind fuck' that jolted me out of my personal thoughts at that point, and I made myself go back into work mode. But I lost it again

before the session was over. And that time it wasn't
something I could gloss over.

♪ ♪ ♪

I went home, uneasy, wanting to talk to Cara. But she'd
already left to go up north for a conference. I had the next
day off so I decided to go fishing.

I hadn't been to the lake in ages. I used to go regularly
with my cousin, then he shifted away so I got out of the
habit. At first, I didn't think it was as much fun on my
own. Now though, I like going alone. It gives me a chance
to think.

I always get up at four o'clock in the morning to go
fishing. It's probably unnecessary: it only takes an hour
and a half to drive to the lake. But whenever my dad took
me fishing as a kid, we would get up at four in the morning.
Fish are at their busiest early, he would say. I have no idea
if he was right, but that was when I believed everything
he said. And despite rubbing my blurry eyes and yawning
every three minutes, I loved the excitement of getting up
so early. When is it we start disbelieving our parents?
When is it we realise their monstrous fallibility? For
the realisation is monstrous. Discovering that a person
you love and adore and depend on can be wrong, or,
worse, can deceive makes the world suddenly much less
safe.

I reached the lake about 5.30 a.m. that day, just before
dawn. It was cold and there was a kind of mist hovering
over the water. I stamped around getting the boat off the

113

trailer, trying to warm up, wanting to disturb the stillness. I was in a positive flurry of activity. Once I'd rowed the boat out to my usual spot, and got out my bait and attached the sinker and cast the line, there was no reason to move around any more, and it seemed so still and quiet. Just me and the fish, waiting, the water lapping at the boat and the grey sky huddled around my shoulders. I sat, very still, very quiet, staring at the surface of the water rippling gently. And I watched the dawn rise up through the mist, like a realisation.

I kept thinking about Vincent. There was something extraordinary there I needed to understand. It itched away at me. I sat in the boat, staring into the green water and replayed our conversations. Underneath it all, that's what I was interested in – what was going on underneath it all. I peered into the gloomy lake water and tried to see the bottom, but there was too much silt swirling. My head felt like it was full of that silt.

As I considered whether I could treat him, I down-played my personal reactions and how I'd lost control and tried to concentrate on the specifics of his case. Even then, I minimised potential obstacles, and persuaded myself that he was more *un*socialised than anti-social and he was open to being modified. But I remained unsure about appropriate and realistic treatment goals. As I look back on my state of mind at that time, I realise that I simply rationalised away my concerns. It was sheer hubris.

I decided I would talk to Jeremy about it when I got back. Not that I really wanted to admit my role in what had happened. It was embarrassing. I hadn't let my guard drop with a client like that for a long time. There's a code of ethics in psychotherapy, and it isn't there for good manners. It's important for the process. And I'd fucked up.

It had happened right at the end of that third session. Vincent got angry at me and I was surprised by it. No excuse, I know, but sudden anger can be a frightening thing, even though I should be used to it by now. It happens in sessions often enough. I have a variety of ways of dealing with it and, if it gets really threatening, there's always the panic button under my desk. But it wasn't that Vincent was violent – not then. He was . . . well, 'angry' doesn't cover it. He was more 'wrathful', the kind of anger which begs for action, which seeks revenge, which reveals a kind of malice.

He had been saying something about his wife, his suspicions, and then he asked, 'What do you think? Do you think she's having an affair?'

Therapists never answer questions like that. You always turn it round again, in the form of another question, like 'What do you think?' That would have done perfectly well. I don't know what I was thinking. Well, yes I do.

'Everything points that way,' I said.

And he erupted, absolutely erupted. His face was right before my face, his eyes wild and round and brimming with hate. I had to gasp, a small sound of air seized.

'And what would you know about it? Is your wife having an affair?'

It was the emotion. I was surprised by it. It shocked the words out of me.

'Yes, I believe she is.'

After that, that gleam of wrath disappeared. It settled into each of us, quiet and still like a sleeping dragon, its fire held within, so we were no longer aware of it. But a silent smoke still rose from its nostrils, dulling my thoughts. I felt stupefied. I felt like someone else – someone with no control, who didn't think, just acted. And so I told him. I even gave him details.

'What's he like?' Vincent had asked.

'He's young. His name's Adrian, he's a drummer in a percussion band.'

'Pulse?'

'Yes,' I said, surprised that he'd heard of it.

Sitting in the boat, waiting for the fish, I remembered and shivered. The green water rippled gently like a silk curtain billowing softly in a breeze. Idiot. Now he knew, he had power over me. The balance had shifted. I was a little frightened. But not as frightened as I should have been. The line twitched and jumped and I quickly reeled it in. My only fish of the morning.

♪ ♪ ♪

Blue

CARA AND I both arrived back late on the Friday night and didn't talk much. We went to bed and I was surprised when she turned to me after the light was out and we had sex. We both came quickly. By the time I got back from the bathroom, she was asleep.

I remember waking late the next morning to see her standing before me, smiling. An aura of sunlight spilled around her. She'd brought me brunch on a tray, complete with a fresh rose, the newspaper and the mail.

'Wake up, sleepyhead. It's almost eleven.'

She kissed me, warm and soft, on the mouth. I remember that kiss so well. It was free of all the overtones, undertones, of everything else that was going on at that time. It was just Cara, and me. It was the last thing I saw clearly.

I had a mouthful of coffee and opened the mail. The letter was one page only, and when I checked the envelope there was no name or return address.

You are not alone

Three Two One

Looking back on it, it's easier to see patterns, to discern explanations for behaviour – both my own and that of others. But at the time it was much less clear. I couldn't think who the letter might be from, or what they were trying to say. It seemed threatening, but vague, the motive puzzling. Could it be Vincent, or some other addled client? There were plenty to choose from. I should have shown it to Cara, or to someone else, but I was rattled.

Usually I think very lucidly. I'm careful about things and I think them through. Once I have a handle on a general concept, then I can deal with the specifics. I suppose that's one of the reasons I dislike conflict. It doesn't give you the opportunity to consider what anyone is saying, let alone yourself. Emotions run higher and higher until the dam just bursts. That's how many people describe it to me – a kind of emotional flooding. Terrifying.

I think that's what was holding me back. Fear of conflict. I can understand these things now. I was trying like mad to understand it at the time – trying too hard, I see now. All those underlying emotions were holding me back from reaching that understanding.

Jeremy tried to help me. He suggested I was trying to explain and analyse my relationship as a way of avoiding it. He was right on the button.

I remember telling him about the time around then that Cara and I had a weekend away on the coast. Cara had suggested it. I needed a break, she said.

M: It was terrible weather and the town was so small, there was nothing to do. Cara kept wanting to go out, but it was pissing down the whole time. I mean, why would you want to go out in that? I said she could go and I stayed in the motel.

J: What did you do?

M: I read – that latest Howard book on relationships. I thought it might help. And I wrote a bit in my journal. I was trying to understand it all, figure stuff out.

J: What were you really doing, Michael?

(*Pause*)

M: I suppose . . . it was a little like I was hiding.

J: What were you hiding from?

(*Pause*)

M: Fear. Anger. Embarrassment.

It was one of those moments in therapy when the patient and therapist feel deeply connected. I actually felt it as a bodily sensation of safety and comfort. It helps, I'm sure, that I'm a therapist too and know where he's going with it all. It lets us get there that much quicker.

I'm almost embarrassed about the way I behaved at that time. I try not to think of it much. Besides, when you look back on the past, everything's distorted. You remember only parts of it, not the whole picture. You emphasise certain things above others, according to your personal construction of truth. I'm trying to leave myself

119

open to questioning and reconsideration, but I have to admit that it's hard to dislodge your initial impressions. If you're feeling jealous, green inevitably colours your views. I know I saw things from a certain viewpoint, in a particular light, and if I'd been standing somewhere slightly more to the left or the right, if I'd switched on another lamp even, things may have looked quite different.

From a psychologist's point of view I find it fascinating. Even the most obvious everyday events can be totally transformed if we are just inventive enough in our constructions. I see this often in my line of work. Ways of thinking determine so much, it's incredible. All mental disorders are characterised by Kant's 'unique private sense of reasoning'. If we don't keep in touch with the world, with 'reality', it's very easy to fall into these little private worlds in which everything is slightly askew. Some, of course, are more askew than others. Some have furniture on the ceiling. Some have no furniture at all. We're influenced not by 'facts' but by our interpretation of them, as Adler says.

Vincent was a classic example. The man had much bigger problems than were initially apparent. I suspected a personality disorder, but in the first few weeks I wasn't sure what. Anti-social, perhaps. He definitely had his own private world, but he was expert at hiding it, or rather, hiding in it. His world was closely related to reality but differed in several marked respects. It wasn't until I stumbled over one of those places that I was able to look around more closely and realise he was somewhere else.

120

It was lucky I knew his GP. I phoned Tom one day to talk about another mutual client and the subject of Vincent came up.

'How's he getting on?' Tom asked.

'Not bad,' I said. 'We've been talking about his parents a lot. And he seems to be getting along better with his wife.'

'His wife? He told me he'd never been married.'

'Are you sure?'

I felt as if I'd just put my arm through one of the walls of Vincent's house.

In our next session, I challenged him on it within the first 10 minutes. He was talking about the institution of marriage.

'I believe you told your doctor you'd never been married,' I said.

He looked me straight in the eye, unfazed. His complete lack of embarrassment almost had me embarrassed.

'Yeah,' he said. There was a pause. Then he grinned at me. 'Yeah. It's easier to tell people that, you know. I just didn't want to go into it all.'

I let it go but I wasn't convinced.

After that session I had a greater wariness about everything Vincent said. I felt that he had a greater wariness too. Like he was watching his feet so he didn't put one wrong. I began to ask more specific questions, to take more notes and compare them later with previous sessions. As it gradually became clear to me just how deluded the man was, I have to admit I was rather impressed. Building such a meticulous and detailed world took real skill. And against my better judgement, I found myself admiring him. In each session I was able to recognise more of his invisible landscape. The more I saw, the more his whole world started to shimmer before me. I wondered how long it would take to collapse. When it did, someone was bound to get hurt. I made the mistake of assuming it would be Vincent.

I never arrange to see my clients outside work. It's simply not professional. I know colleagues who have got into terrible messes by having other kinds of relationships with their clients. However, sometimes you can't help running into clients socially. One night I met Vincent. Now I wonder whether it really was by accident, although I can't see any way he could have known I was going to be there.

I was invited by a couple of colleagues to go to a lecture by a visiting psychologist. I didn't know who or what the topic was before I arrived. I'd simply met David and Stephanie after work for a drink and decided to tag along when they said they were going. The lecture turned out to be about the psychology of music.

I probably wouldn't have gone to it on my own, but I did find the subject interesting at first. The speaker, Dr Wanda Cottington, was giving a theoretical account of the emotional response to music, presenting a new model based on four basic assumptions: music is heard as sound; as human utterance; as narrative; and in context. 'I will attempt,' she said, 'to illustrate how a conception of emotional response to music in these terms can lead to a model that is generic enough to be independent of the idiosyncrasies of individuals and musical styles, but concrete enough to allow considerable predictive power.'

I'm afraid I stopped listening after that. I started thinking about Cara's new-found interest in music and sat dreaming for the rest of the talk, thinking of her and Adrian.

I was still distracted during the wine and cheese part of the evening. I stood with David and Stephanie, adding little to their chatter. It gave me a shock when I turned back to them and there was Vincent beside us.

'Hello Michael.'

It threw me. He was very good at that, Vincent. For some reason when I introduced him to David and Stephanie, I didn't mention he was a client. We talked about the lecture.

'Are you a therapist, Vincent?' asked Stephanie.

'No, no,' he said, and smiled at me. 'But I am interested in music.'

That was news to me.

'Ah. So what's the music-lover's point of view? Do you think Wanda's thesis valid?' Stephanie asked.

'It seemed to me an extremely long explanation of what is simple common sense.'

'How do you mean?'

'All that stuff in the second half about whether emotional responses are central to the experience of music – anyone who has ever been to a concert can tell you that.'

'And?'

'Have you people never heard Shostakovich's Fifth symphony? The third movement is pure grief. For loss and longing, take Tchaikovsky's Swan Lake. Bach's double violin concerto: peace and serenity. Happiness: pretty much any Mozart.'

I stepped back and watched Vincent explain himself to the others. Soon another couple joined us and they were just as interested in his exposition. He was very smooth, a bit too slick perhaps. He was being deliberately provocative, but with style. You could see people reacting against him while simultaneously falling under his influence. After a burst of loud laughter from our group, Dr Wanda Cottington came over.

'So nice to see people enjoying themselves at these things. What's the joke?'

'One of us seems to think people would be just as well off listening to Mozart as visiting a therapist.'

'Ah, an altogether different Mozart effect! Interesting. There are, of course, a range of music therapies. Music and psychoanalysis overlap significantly in the domain of emotion and the necessity for engaged listening. There is no escape from hearing, after all – unlike the eye, the ear cannot be wilfully closed.'

I decided to prove her wrong. I said a discreet farewell to Stephanie and tried to slip away quietly. But Vincent followed me towards the door and took my arm.

'I met a friend of yours the other day,' he said.

'Oh yes,' I said warily.

'Like I said, I'm into music.'

'And?'

'And I went to see Pulse.'

I felt instantly cold. I spoke too quickly.

'Why did you do that?'

'I just thought I'd check out this Adrian guy.'

'You really shouldn't have done that.'

'But we're friends, Doc. Your problems are my problems.'

And vice versa, so it seemed. My legs started to shake. I couldn't stand his smile, the way his eyes stared at me so relentlessly, without blinking. What had I got myself into?

'I've got to get going.'

I hurried out of the room and ran all the way down the stairs and into the carpark. My fingers fumbled my keys and I dropped them by the car. As I picked them up, I bumped my head on the side mirror and swore. Everything was happening too fast. I had to calm down. I had to work this out. I drove home in half the normal time. It was as if I was trying to escape from much more than Vincent.

♪ ♪ ♪

Indigo

FOR THE next week I was anxious to see Vincent again, but I persuaded myself not to ring, just to wait and mention Adrian casually during the next session. Only he didn't turn up. I could tell after the first 10 minutes that he wasn't going to come. I spent the rest of the hour wondering what to do, if I should call him, where he was, what he was doing. Was he stalking Adrian even now? This was exactly why therapists never got involved with clients, never divulged personal information. I'd have to tell someone now. I'd been meaning to tell Jeremy, but I'd chickened out. How could I tell Jeremy without admitting what I'd told Vincent?

I was completely distracted for the rest of the day. My next appointment was with a university lecturer. It took me a while to tune into him. He was very indignant at the beginning of the session, expressing annoyance at some of his students for showing up late to tutorials.

'I hate to be late,' he said. 'I can't understand how they can be so blasé about it. Can't they see it's a sign of respect to be on time? I always make sure I'm on time for appointments. In fact I hurried especially to arrive here punctually today.'

I wondered at the emphasis and woke up a little.

'I wonder if I've left you feeling disrespected here somehow,' I said.

There was a pause.

There you go again, I thought. Idiot.

'Well, yes,' he said. Wow. 'The last two weeks you've started our sessions three minutes late.'

Three minutes! I bit my tongue.

'I suppose I've been wondering if what I have to say has been boring you,' he admitted.

So there we are. The desire for affirmation. If I valued him I'd be on time. Of course it was nothing to do with him, but everyone's self-obsessed. I had to swallow my impatience. Still, he reminded me of a valuable lesson. We need not just to talk about love, we need to demonstrate it.

I went home that night and made dinner. It was simple: spaghetti bolognese, one of the three meals I can make. But I set the table, put flowers in a vase, made a salad and put out some fresh bread. Cara came in later than I expected.

'Where've you been?'

'An early movie.'

She leaned over to kiss me and I smelt a new perfume,

128

felt the imprint of her indigo lipstick on my cheek.

'Who with?'

She turned her back to me, fiddling with her handbag.

'Adrian.'

'And Lissa?'

'No, just Adrian.'

Cara turned round and looked straight at me.

'Is that all right?' she asked.

It was one of those rare moments that I instantly recognised as an opportunity, a turning point. What I say here is important, I thought, and I felt a sudden clarity, a lightening, as if my mind had been wiped clear. I looked directly into her hazel-brown eyes and smiled.

'Yes,' I said. 'That's perfectly all right.'

We sat and ate dinner together. We didn't talk much. It felt like there was a kind of peace between us. I forgot about Vincent. I even forgot about Adrian. And afterwards she said thank you.

'I get sick of cooking sometimes.'

'Do you? I thought you enjoyed it.'

'Usually. Just sometimes lately it's felt a bit like hard work.'

'We should go away on a proper holiday somewhere, just the two of us.'

'Hmmmm.'

I didn't let her pull back this time.

'Would you like to do that?'

'I'm not sure. I'll think about it.'

'We could even go overseas if you like – Australia, Hong Kong, one of the islands.'

'Mmm. Maybe.'

'How do you feel about that?'

'I don't know! All right? I don't want to think about how I feel at the moment.'

Too far.

'Sorry,' I said.

I can see how it might be difficult living with a therapist. I cleared away the dishes and Cara went and lay on the couch. Later, I was in my study, sending emails, when she came in.

'Want some coffee?' she asked.

'Thanks.'

'Sorry I was a grump. I think I do need a break.'

'So how would you feel about going away somewhere?'

'It's okay with me.'

'That's not a feeling.'

She tried again. 'It sounds good.'

'Still not a feeling,' I said.

'Aaaaaaagh!' She put her hands round my throat and pretended to throttle me.

'I feel, I feel, I feel . . . like . . .'

She pushed me back in my chair and sat on my lap, relaxed her hands around my neck into an embrace.

'I love you,' she said, smiling. 'Is that enough of a feeling for you?'

'Oh yeah,' I said, leaning her back and kissing her. 'That's a great feeling.'

♪ ♪ ♪

The next day I decided to come home early from work, surprise Cara. Afterwards I couldn't help thinking about how events depend on so many little decisions like that. What if I hadn't decided to come home early? What if I had decided to go for a drink instead, or catch up on some paperwork at the office? What if I'd got a flat tyre coming home, or was delayed by a road accident? What if, what if . . . It can drive you mad. You can follow the 'what if' trajectory too far; after all, that's not your life. Your life is the 'what'; forget the bloody 'if'.

Anyway, I came home early. As I drove up the drive, I caught a glimpse of a movement out of the corner of my eye. I stopped short of the garage and walked to the front door instead of using the internal access. I walked slowly, my heart beating hard. I could feel my right eye start up with a tic that I used to get when nervous. The red-leaved shrubs along the side of the property are hardly tall enough to be called a hedge. It was quite clear he was crouching behind them. This was too much.

I stopped and took a deep breath. I looked around desperately for anything I could use if he turned violent. A small spade lay next to the flower bed on the far side of the door. I quickly calculated how many steps it would take me to reach it, or whether he would seize it first. My mouth flooded with saliva.

'Vincent,' I said. It came out in a croak.

He stood up slowly, grinning. Again, completely at ease. Nothing fazed the man.

I tried not to look at the spade.

'What are you doing here?' I asked, in a stronger voice.

131

At least he wasn't making any sudden moves. I figured the most dangerous time was past; Cara didn't seem to be home and I'd taken him by surprise. I walked casually over to the garden bed, closer to the spade. The hose was in the corner and I thought I could always grab that too if necessary. Throughout, I watched Vincent intently. His eyes had narrowed and a smile played around his wet, pink lips. There was no time for 'what ifs' then. I had to concentrate.

'Hey, Doc,' he said, cheerily. 'Just thought I'd pop round.'

'And why are you hiding in my hedge?'

He laughed. Still no shame.

'Just being discreet.'

'You shouldn't come to my home, Vincent. If you need to see me, you can make an appointment at my office.'

How the hell had he found out where I lived anyway? I was always careful about those things – nothing was listed. I remembered the strange letter.

'I just wanted to talk to you right away.'

'Let's go back to the office then. I can take you in my car.'

I wanted to get him away from my house, away from Cara. How could I have put her in danger like this? It had to stop. I felt like weeping.

'No, it's okay, Doc. I can wait till tomorrow. I'll ring your office.'

He came out of the hedge towards me. I felt a sudden urgency to keep hold of him, to know exactly where he was.

132

'If it was important enough for you to come here, Vincent, it's important enough for us to discuss it now.'

He hesitated.

'Let's go then,' he said.

I asked for us to drive in silence; I wanted to think. My plan formed as I drove. There was one dicey moment when he realised we weren't going towards my rooms and I saw his hands grip the sides of his seat.

'Where are we going? I thought we were going to your office?'

'We are,' I said. 'I've just got to pick up some things from my rooms at the hospital.'

'I didn't know you had an office at the hospital.'

'Oh yes, I'm a consultant there, but I don't use the rooms much. Don't worry, it won't take long.'

It was surprisingly simple. I knew there would be security at the hospital reception, and after my hurried, whispered explanation they swung into action and restrained him. It took him a moment to realise what was happening, then he started yelling like a madman. Very helpful, considering. At least they would be able to hold him for a couple of days. It was the first step towards my plan of getting him committed.

It felt good. I didn't care that it was hypocritical. I didn't care that I had pledged to stand by him as a client. He had threatened my personal world and I wanted to be rid of him.

I didn't tell Cara. I should have. We had too many secrets. But the explanation would have involved too many layers, revelations I wasn't ready for. I wasn't ready for much at that point. I was so shocked by it all. It was as if I had been physically attacked. I lay in bed that night with Cara sleeping peacefully beside me and I couldn't stop shaking. I was shaking with anger. I wasn't angry with myself – although I should have been. I wasn't even angry at Vincent. I was livid with Adrian.

♪ ♪ ♪

Violet

STILL, I woke up feeling more clear-headed than I had in weeks. I sang in the shower. I made myself a good, fatty breakfast of bacon and eggs. I read the paper slowly and closed it with a certain satisfaction, gazed out the window at the morning sun glinting off the wet trees, and just sat and looked for a minute. It was beautiful. I remember thinking that. Everything seemed slower, sharper. I was noticing the world again.

I tried not to think of Vincent. It had been so simple to get him into hospital, into somebody else's hands. Too simple, really. I didn't want to think about what would happen next. I didn't want to dwell on culpability. I refused to look any further into Vincent's world, which so easily could be transformed into my own.

In some ways Vincent reminded me of my father. Not

that my father was a sociopath, but he was different from who he appeared to be. He was concerned with appearances, with the way other people perceived him. And yet he had his own little world in which he was quite a different person. How shocked I was when I first caught him in women's clothing.

That morning, the phone rang as I stood in front of the mirror tying a tie. I had to go to a seminar and needed to look the part: charcoal jacket and pressed trousers, dark shirt and dark tie. I am more authoritative with a tie – it's not just that I feel it, I *am* more authoritative. That small slip of material has a latent power. It lies there against my chest and says to all who see it, I belong, I am accepted. It comforts me, that tie. It doesn't matter how I feel behind it. I can be nervous, doubtful, ignorant even. The tie protects me. Perhaps I am like my father.

I looked at myself standing there before the mirror and remembered how I used to watch my father do the same thing, getting dressed, tying his tie. If a small boy was standing by the bed looking at me at that moment, he would have seen a man very like my father when he was in his forties – smart clothes, tall, black hair greying at the temples and smoothed back, a somewhat craggy face, clean-shaven, blue eyes with a touch of sadness in them and a touch of something else I can't quite say. Still, I'm not like my father in any real way. I'm not like him at all.

The tie wasn't knotting properly. I cursed quietly and undid it.

Once I'd finished dressing, I went down to my study to get my briefcase. I was going past the living-room

136

when I heard a strange sound. I looked in and there was Cara sitting on the floor, with her arms wrapped around her knees, her shoulders jerking from harsh, wild sobs. I remembered the phone ringing. Adrian, I thought. What has he done? I wasn't sure what to do. There was a split second when I almost kept walking towards my study, but I made myself go in and sit down beside her.

'What's happened?'

She grabbed my arm and pulled me to her, her face red and distorted as if under water. I felt helpless. I stroked her long brown hair, stroked and stroked.

'James,' she choked.

Her stepfather had died.

How strange that I had just been thinking about my own father.

Cara wouldn't let me drive her up to her mother's place. She said she needed time with her family. I understood. I said I'd come up for the funeral. It gave me a few days to get sorted at work. And I had to go see the hospital psych team again about Vincent. It would soon become hard to keep him in hospital. He was a plausible bastard, I'll give him that. I tried to make my story equally plausible. I told the doctors he was a threat to himself. I even falsified a couple of records. It scares me now to realise how interwoven I became in his web.

I drove up to Riverton trying to forget Vincent. Driving was soothing; I was glad to feel in control again. When I got to the house where Cara's mother lived, a house like all the other houses in the street, a small box of a house with white weatherboards and net curtains, I didn't want to stop. But I pulled into the driveway, paused for 30 seconds, no more, and got out. Cara opened the front door and came out to the car, her shoes crunching loudly on the gravel drive. She stood before me, close, her nose almost under my chin, her reddened eyes on my throat, hands wrapped tight under each arm. It felt as if I hadn't seen her in weeks. I wondered if Adrian saw her like this. If he noticed the sparks of red buried in her chestnut-brown hair and flaring up under the sun; if he looked closely enough to see the tiny fine lines appearing under her deep brown eyes; saw the way she held herself, head tilted to the right, looking at the world on her own private angle.

She looked exhausted. She had a look of calmness, spent acceptance.

'Michael,' she said. It sounded like a decision.

I put my arms around her and felt the bones in her narrow shoulders, smelt her perfume. She was my wife. I wanted so much to comfort her, to be her succour, her protector, her haven.

'Everything will be all right,' I said.

She held me tight and pressed her forehead into my chest, as if finding my heartbeat. She stood there for a minute and listened. Then we broke apart, and went inside.

Elizabeth was in the kitchen with Eve, making scones.

'Michael, how nice to see you. Thank you for coming.'

I shook her hand. No one hugs Elizabeth.

'I'm so sorry, Elizabeth.'

She pressed my hand and smiled. She had Cara's uneven smile or Cara had hers: lips closed, turned up at the ends in a concession of a smile, an allowance, more for your benefit than hers. Still she looked good, she looked fine.

Eve gave me a hug without waiting.

'Hi sweetie,' she said.

I always liked Eve. She's Cara's younger sister, outwardly quite different from Cara: shorter, with blue eyes, cropped brown hair, a tiny nose-piercing, very outgoing, confident.

'How are you, Eve?'

'We're doing all right, aren't we, Mum?

'We certainly are.'

Cara left the room some time around then, though I didn't notice immediately.

'Would you like a scone, Michael?'

'Thanks. They look great.'

'We're making three dozen for this afternoon. I have no idea how many to make. I mean, how do you know how many people will come to a funeral? At least it's a fine day so there's not the excuse of the weather.'

'I think Cara's rather pipped we wouldn't let her help,' said Eve. 'But she's arranged the rest of the catering so it's only fair we get to do something ourselves.'

I remembered Cara complaining on the phone about Eve not doing anything towards the organisation.

'When did you arrive?' I asked.

'Wednesday night. Have you seen the lounge? Absolutely stuffed full of flowers. You can't go in without sneezing.'

She bent to lift a sheet of scones out of the oven.

Elizabeth came and stood next to me, that little upturned smile again, as if she had something to say.

'I'm glad you're here, Michael, for Cara.'

'I couldn't not come. You're family.'

Elizabeth nodded, a short bob of her head, a small wrinkle between her eyes.

'Cara seems rather . . . emotional.' She frowned more deeply. Elizabeth was wary about emotions. 'I'm not sure what . . . You need to help her.'

I was surprised at her request.

'I'm sure it's just grief, Elizabeth.'

I shouldn't have said 'just'.

'Yes.' She nodded again. 'She seems different, that's all.'

You seem different too, I thought.

Elizabeth had never talked to me like this before, so personally. She seemed to me a strict person, very strict on others and on herself. She lived in a very orderly way. She had standards. I liked that about her. Cara had told me she hadn't always been like that. When she was with Eddie, Cara and Eve's father, 'Things were much more fluid,' Cara had said. 'Then she met James and got it together.' Perhaps now James was gone she was reverting. Grief can loosen you up.

I touched her on the shoulder. She looked surprised but not annoyed.

'She's working things out,' I said. 'She's working out what's important to her, what she needs.'

Eve was looking at me strangely.

'I'll go see how she is,' I said.

140

I found Cara in the hallway, putting on her coat.

'Let's go for a walk.'

We went down to the river and walked along its damp banks, our shoes pulling slightly in the mud. For a while Cara talked about Eve, complaining again. They always rubbed each other up the wrong way, those two. Each was a little envious of the other's qualities, and they reacted against that. Then she started talking about her mother. I was surprised at how angry she was.

'I can't believe how uncaring she is. It seems like she's moved on already. I was helping her pack away James's things the other day and she was quite cheerful about it – just lumped all his clothes in a bag to give to the Cancer Society without even looking at them. You'd think she'd want to go through his stuff, keep some things maybe.'

'What for?'

'I don't know, she could have given some to you, or something.'

'I don't need anything.'

'I know you don't need anything! I just think she should stop for a minute and think about what she's doing, think about James. He was so important for her. He gave her stability, security. What's she going to do now?'

'She seems to be coping well. She's much more open than I remember.'

'That's what I mean! She's changing. She's lost her anchor.'

She stopped and looked at the river. 'Everybody needs an anchor,' she whispered.

I stood behind her.

'What are you afraid of, Cara?'

'I'm afraid of her drifting off, losing control of her life. She was talking about freedom last night. She's excited, for God's sake! I said to her, "Mum, you always had freedom. You had plenty of freedom with Michael."'

'Michael?'

'James. I mean James.'

She squatted down on the riverbank, pushed her fingers into the wet earth angrily.

'She was all over the place before James. James gave her discipline. If she loses that, she really will lose her freedom.'

She was almost crying.

'Why are you so angry, Car?'

I was bewildered. I hated seeing her hurting.

'We all get angry sometimes.'

She stood up abruptly and looked me in the eye.

'*You've* been angry lately.'

'Have I?'

'Yes. Why are you so angry?'

There was a challenge in her eyes. I didn't know what to say. It started to rain. Her face crumpled and she reached up for me blindly, clung to me; the breath pushed out of her small body, wheezed in, squeezed out, over and over, like a bellows. I hugged her hard. I would do anything to not have her hurting. She could have him if he made her happy. That's all I wanted.

Later that afternoon, during the funeral, I was afraid I wouldn't be able to help her when she needed it. She sat next to me during the service, her hand on mine, as tight as a lid. She'd dressed well – a new black dress, stockings, her best black high heels – but she hadn't any make-up on, and her face looked worn, two patches of violet swelling under her eyes as if someone had hit her. Grief. I knew it was healthy but I still wanted so much to make it stop. She sat there crying while her mother was speaking, little rivulets of salty liquid trickling down her face like ice melting. She looked up at me at one point. I put one arm around her shoulder and the other across her chest and joined them together in a circle. I felt the love transfer in the beat of my heart, in my breath, in the pulse of my thoughts. She calmed. She leaned against me. She let me take her weight and closed her eyes.

I don't remember the rest of the service very well. It seemed no time at all before we were out in the dark afternoon, standing around that hole, gaping obscenely at the rain-spattered ground waiting to receive James.

We had turned to go when Cara stopped. She touched my arm and pointed. Her face was turned up, her smile as beautiful as a baby's. 'Look!' she said and pointed again.

The hills were covered with brooding charcoal clouds. Above, in a gap of sky, a slim rainbow hovered, its colours a thin sweep of memory. Life. Cara clutched on to one end and I took the other.

♪ ♪ ♪

Allegro

IT'S STRANGE to think now about what happened. For a while, I deliberately chose not to think about it. I didn't talk about it either. Not to anybody. I wanted to sometimes, but to put it into words was too difficult, and would have given it more substance than I was willing to admit. It's like sometimes you do things and you don't know why, and you don't really try to find out why, because you don't want to know. You really know, though. You know. You just don't want to think about it.

The first time I saw Adrian on stage was at the Opera House. I think of it every time I go there to see anything – a play, a dance, an opera – I think of sitting there in the front row of the circle, watching his bare chest shimmer in a slick of sweat, his quick breaths raising his ribs like piano keys depressed and released. I remember closing my eyes and feeling the drumbeat slam into my feet and shudder through the surface of my skin.

I had gone with Melissa, who was six months pregnant.

'That was definitely a mistake,' she said at half-time. Her baby had hated it, or loved it: hard to tell. It had banged against the walls of her uterus the entire time, a small tangible echo.

'It must seem like a giant heartbeat,' said Liss.

We met Adrian's mother out on the balcony. Later, I wished I'd taken more notice of her. She was nervous, clutching a cigarette in one hand and a glass of wine in the other. She didn't look much like Adrian – he must've taken after his father. I never met him. He was long gone. That was another thing we had in common – fathers who left. His mother was large, her upper arms bulging tight against the thin silky fabric of her shirt and the loose skin of her neck hanging in folds like a boxer dog's jowls. Her face lifted in a wide smile as she saw Melissa.

'Thank God, I know someone here. Starting to show, dear. When are you due?'

'A few more months to go. This is my friend Cara.'

'Barbara. What did you think of the first half? Loud, wasn't it? Adrian said I'd like the second half better, but I think he just said that to make sure I sat through the whole thing.'

She had a laugh like birdsong, a light, rippling crescendo.

'Adrian's great,' I said. 'All that energy.'

'Yes, he's always been a bit manic,' she said, touching

my hand in a friendly way. I'm always shocked when strangers touch me. 'I used to worry about him. He would bang the pots and pans just like that when he was two years old, and he hasn't stopped since. We even had to get our doorbell taken out because he wouldn't stop ringing it.'

The bird sang again.

Later, I recounted the story to Adrian and he told me it wasn't true, that his mother liked to exaggerate. I wasn't sure who to believe, but Barbara appeared more credible. It seemed Adrian couldn't remember much about his childhood – he never talked about it anyway. Besides, I could just imagine him as a little boy, standing on tiptoe, reaching out a skinny arm to press the button over and over again.

We all sat together for the second half and, next to me, Barbara kept giggling. Adrian had been right – she did like the second half better. So did I. The water piece especially. They filled up earthen pots and trickled, dripped and poured it into buckets and wooden containers. The sound of water. I closed my eyes and listened to the gurgling fountain of music. Patterns trickled together to form pictures: a clear mountain stream running cold with melted snow, rain plopping on the leaves of a giant gunnera plant, the shush-shush of the tide creeping in.

'It just made me want to pee,' said Melissa, rushing to the loo at the end.

We met Adrian afterwards at a late-night café across the road. When we first shook hands he took off his glasses and I remember being shocked by the blue of his eyes. Sea blue. Against his dark eyebrows and the dark brown fringe that fell across his face, his blue eyes were as startling as if they had been pink. He smiled. I almost smiled back.

Adrian was shorter than he appeared on stage, with broad shoulders and a tight torso. There was a tidiness about him, as if his body had been carefully packaged. I came to be jealous of the easy way he held himself – he had a dancer's casual awareness of his body and often expressed himself through small movements. It seemed quite unconscious most of the time, but if he was unsure about something you could see it in one of his knees jiggling up and down, like notes vibrating on a string instrument. I liked his physicality. There was a sense of power behind it. He seemed a lot surer of his grip on the earth than I was. I used to think of him as more 'in sync'.

That first night he was a terrible flirt. At the café, Melissa had motioned him over to join us.

'You remember Cara?'

'Of course. How could I forget?'

He kissed the hand I held out. I blushed. *I* had forgotten.

'Have we met?'

'Cara!' Lissa sputtered. 'Don't you remember? I brought Adrian to your wedding.'

'Oh. Yes. You look different.'

I hardly remembered Lissa's partner at the wedding. I had been in a daze all that day.

150

'Older probably,' he said.

'You're not even 30,' said Lissa, poking his stomach. 'Hey, you've lost weight.'

'It's all that running round on stage. I'm starting to miss my slothful composing days.'

'Well, it's good for your figure, hon, as well as your wallet. Speaking of which, go get us some more coffee.'

'Rude cow. Cara, what can I get you?'

As he went to the counter, Lissa raised an eyebrow at me and drained her cup.

'What?' I asked, a little defensive.

'I'd watch out if I were you.'

'Why?'

'The hand thing. I can always tell when Adrian gets his eye on someone. He kisses their hand.'

'Get off. He probably does it to all the girls.'

'Oh no, darling, not everyone. Only the ones he wants to start with kissing their hands and continue up their arms and down to their . . .'

'Shut up.'

Lissa snorted.

'I can't believe you didn't remember him. I used to talk about him all the time – must've thought I was in lurve.'

'Were you?'

'Nah, just charmed. Literally charmed the pants off me. Before I found out what he was really like.'

'Do you think I offended him?'

'What, by forgetting who he was? It'll take more than that to put him off. Look at him.'

Adrian was standing at the counter, waiting for the

coffee and looking back at us, smiling sexily. Lissa went over to give him a hand and said something that made him smile even more. I looked for something in my handbag. I'd forgotten what it was like to be looked at in that way.

Peter arrived just as they sat down.

'Hey guys. Good show?'

'Good audience anyway,' said Adrian.

'Great. We better go, Liss, I'm double-parked.'

'But we just got another coffee.'

'You shouldn't be drinking coffee anyway. Junior's hands will come out shaking. Come on, it's late and we've got an early start tomorrow.'

Lissa got up, grumbling, and they said their goodbyes.

'I really should get going too,' I said.

'They're just turning into parents already,' said Adrian. 'Besides, I was about to buy you the most enormous piece of chocolate cake.'

I objected half-heartedly, but somehow he persuaded me to eat it with him. It felt like we'd known each other for ages.

'Sorry I didn't recognise you from the wedding,' I said. 'I was really vague that day.'

'Getting married does that, I guess.'

'You're not married?'

'Not likely.'

'I had totally cold feet.'

'Really? It didn't look like it.'

'God, yes. All the way up the aisle I was still wondering if I could go through with it.'

'No one would have known it. You looked the perfect bride, lovely and in love.'

'Well, in love anyway.'

I smiled as I remembered. Those days had been so blissful.

'Where is your husband tonight?'

'Up north, at a conference. He's giving a paper on obsessive-compulsive disorders. One of his clients washes his hands 600 times a day, literally 600 times. After every little thing he does, he has to wash his hands.'

'Amazing what the mind makes us think we have to do.'

'The trick is resisting it,' I said. I wondered what *he* felt he had to do.

He smiled again, a mischievous, crooked smile.

'Sometimes it's better to go with your instincts.'

I finished my coffee.

'Like music,' he continued. 'With music you always have to go with your instincts. Let go and see what happens.'

I see now that this was one of the things that drew me to Adrian. He seemed like one of those people who could 'let go'. I wasn't. Perhaps that's something he taught me to do. He was wrong, though – it isn't always best. Sometimes what happens is not at all what you expect.

'Not that I've been doing much composing lately. I seem to be in a performance-only phase at the moment. I'm missing something I need.'

'What do you need?'

His mouth softened.

'Faith.' He shrugged. 'It'll come back.

'Were any of those pieces tonight by you?'

'Yeah, the water one.'

'That was my favourite.'

Something in his face changed, like the shudder of a flower beginning to unfold.

'Really?'

'Absolutely. I'm not just saying it.'

'Maybe I better get writing some more then.'

The waitress came and cleared away our empty cups. She looked at us, stifling a yawn. 'Anything else?'

'No thanks,' I said and reached for my jacket. 'I really should get going.'

'Can I grab a lift off you?'

'Sure. Where are you going?'

'The east side of town.'

We gathered our things and walked to the car. Adrian walked with a swing to his step, the carefree ease of a cat. I felt clumsy beside him. On the drive to his house I asked more about his music. He'd begun playing the xylophone in primary school and had gone on to drums as a teenager. 'Your poor mother,' I said. At university he got into gamelan. I pretended I knew what it was. Then composing. He'd met the other members of Pulse when they asked if they could perform some of his pieces, and he joined the group a few months later.

'I love it. It's becoming more physical, though. Our manager says we need more than the music, we need to put on a show. I don't know. It's fun, I guess.'

'What do you think about when you do it?'

'Nothing.'

I loved that. He didn't 'think', he just *was*. That was so Adrian. He never seemed to analyse feelings – his own or anyone else's; he just was happy, was sad, was whatever. He never asked why. Michael asked me once if Adrian even knew what he was feeling. 'Of course he does,' I said indignantly. Now that I think about it again, I think yes, he did know. He knew what he was feeling, but I don't think he knew why. Perhaps it's better not to know why.

There weren't any carparks outside his house, so I pulled up in a driveway.

'You could park in the alleyway and come in for a drink,' he said.

'No, I better not, thanks.'

In the light of the street lamps, his face looked all sharp angles. I wondered what he was doing even as he was kissing me.

'Good night.'

And he was gone, leaving me still wondering.

♪ ♪ ♪

Andante

I'M STILL not sure what I thought I was doing. Maybe it was about freedom. Probably it was about control. Freedom depends on control – Adrian said that once. He was trying to explain to me the importance of discipline in music. We were talking about spontaneity in perform- ance, and he said impulsive expression on its own just produced a 'mess'. Mastery of pitch and other musical controls were necessary before the freedom of spontaneity.

I didn't really get it at the time. All I knew was I wanted to play. I tried to talk to Melissa about it, but she wasn't very receptive back then, she'd just had her baby after all and Ellie was the new centre of her world. She couldn't talk of anything else, she couldn't think of anything else, she had eyes only for Ellie. It was like she had a new lover. I remember watching them as they gazed at each other and wondering at the love between them. It was hard not to be jealous.

'So how was the birth, really?'

Lissa looked up from the little bundle in her arms and laughed softly.

'Don't ask such things!'

'But I want to know. I'm not saying I want a child, not immediately, not yet. But maybe one day and I want to know what it's like. Is it really the worst pain in the world?'

'Let me put down Ellie and I'll get us a cuppa.'

I watched as she gently set the baby down in the bassinet in the corner of the room. She looked at Ellie dreamily then turned and smiled at me, her eyes closing briefly, and I glimpsed her exhaustion. Tears sprang to my eyes, surprising me for the second time that day – my eyes had also filled when I saw Ellie. She had such beautiful miniature hands, perfect slender fingers with tiny pale moons for nails. I had gazed at her small wrinkled face and felt awe.

'What's it like being a mother?'

The doorbell went. Lissa blinked and stared at me, a misty look on her face.

'It's like I'm beginning to understand what love is.'

She went to answer the door and I stood in the middle of the room and felt like crying. She came back in with Cecily, exclaiming over the cooked dinners she'd brought over. Cecily had twins.

'Food is absolutely the best present at the moment,' Lissa said. 'Parents always know.'

I glanced at the woollen booties and hat I had brought, and that sat discarded on the floor.

'Perhaps I should go,' I said.

'No, no, you haven't even had a hold yet,' said Lissa. 'Look, she's still awake. Why don't you pick her up?'

She turned to Cecily and brought out some contraption designed to pump breast milk. I shuddered and went over to the bassinet. Such a round face, such tiny limbs. Ellie was remarkably intimidating for so small a creature. I tried to remember how to pick up a baby. The head, watch the head. Somehow I managed to get her into my arms. I held her gingerly, as if she was bone china.

The doorbell went again. This time it was Adrian. Lissa went off to the loo and I showed him the baby.

'Jesus,' he said, stepping back. I couldn't help giggling. He said something about bringing a curry. How did everyone but me know to bring food? Ellie started to cry. Luckily, Cecily came over and took her from me.

Adrian and I stayed by the windows, looking out over the garden. He poured me some more tea. I felt inexplicably grateful as he handed me the cup. Lissa reappeared and began talking to Cecily about breastfeeding. I have no idea what I said to Adrian, no idea what he said to me. All I know is that by the time I went out the front door again we were going out on Saturday night.

♪ ♪ ♪

I guess that was our first proper date. The symphony orchestra. Now that I come to think of it, almost every time we went out together music was involved somehow. There were the orchestral concerts, the percussion and drumming groups, jazz, opera, rock, then the dancing, Latin American, clubbing. I wasn't used to any of it. Especially clubbing. I felt too old. Yet, in a way, that's what I liked about it. It wasn't until we went to a nightclub that I began to worry about whether we were going out as anything more than friends.

I remember the first time we went clubbing. We had met for a drink and gone to a movie. I'm sure Adrian had no idea what was playing that night. I can't believe he actually wanted to see the new version of *Anna Karenina*. But then he could always surprise me. The film wasn't so bad. It was just the grim ending that got to me. Afterwards I asked Adrian what he thought and he shrugged a bit and suggested we grab some coffee to perk us up.

'It was a bit heavy, wasn't it?' I said.

'Tell you what, a new club opened last week, round the corner. Let's go check it out.'

'I think I'd rather have coffee.'

'We can have coffee in the lounge there. It won't be pumping yet, not before midnight.'

Somehow he managed to talk me into it. Adrian was right, there weren't that many people there, but it was loud, way too loud. He bought me a whisky as well as a short black and we sat in the big leather seats in the 'lounge' part of the club. We could hardly hear one another. I had to keep asking Adrian to repeat himself

160

and he had to keep leaning towards me to speak into my ear. I could feel the brush of his cheek against my hair and it made the side of my face tingle. I still couldn't hear, but I nodded and laughed and pretended that I could. It was probably the whisky.

He was telling me about one of the DJs who worked there and I sat back and watched him talking. His eyes were striking. Adrian had a way of looking at you when he was talking, as though all his attention was focused on you. I'm sure I wasn't the only person he had that effect on. He tried to get a lot of people to love him; it wasn't just me. At the time, though, I liked the way he talked to me, as if he was really interested. I even let him drag me up onto the dance floor. As we crashed back down on the leather couches, I felt his bare arm sweaty against my own. I thought, This is what hope feels like.

♪ ♪ ♪

Stringendo

I KNOW Michael blames himself. When he's not blaming Adrian. I'm still waiting for him to blame me. I guess Michael didn't help, working all those long hours, leaving me feeling unloved. And Adrian certainly went all out: I got the full force of his charm, a force not to be underestimated. But it wasn't just that. It was the whole thing. Like, the music.

One of the nights Michael was out, I sat home alone, feeling sorry for myself, listening to music. It was windy. Gusts kept shaking the windows like someone wanting to get in. It made me feel edgy, weak, as if I might break down for no reason at all.

I put on the Pulse CD I'd bought after that first show. The music had a face now, a dance, a mischievous grin. But if I closed my eyes and concentrated, I was left with the drumbeat. It beat, beat, beat at me, insistent that I remember. What did it remind me of? I sat and listened for ages, trying to find the memory.

'Why are you sitting in the dark?' Michael said, when he finally got home. I don't know how long I'd been there.

'The bulb's gone.'

He flicked the switch by the door and light flooded the room, making me blink.

'Obviously,' he said.

'I thought it had,' I said. 'Anyway, I'm going to bed.'

Michael checked his watch and looked at me in that way he has, when he's concerned about something and trying not to appear so.

'I haven't made dinner,' I said. 'Help yourself to whatever's in the fridge.'

Now he didn't even try to disguise it.

'Are you okay, Cara?'

'That time of the month. I'm going to bed.'

It *was* that time of the month, but I don't know if that had anything to do with it. I was just tired. Tired of having to look after Michael as well as myself. Tired of my job. It had been one of those hard days. Some days I couldn't help screening out, seeing the radiography patients as bodies rather than people. I wanted a change. I didn't know what I wanted. Whatever it was, I was going to seek it out.

♪ ♪ ♪

Lissa rang the next morning.

'We're going up to the beach house this weekend with a few friends to celebrate our wedding anniversary. Would you and Michael like to come?'

'Yes,' I said, without stopping to think. 'Yes, we'd love to.'

I asked Michael that evening as I was washing salad vegetables. I watched the water flow over my hands, feeling the coldness. He didn't answer immediately. I turned off the tap and shook drops of water from the lettuce, and heard the shoosh-shoosh of the leaves and the water through the air. I almost forgot what we'd been talking about.

'Yes,' said Michael. 'Why don't we?'

'Why don't we what?'

'Why don't we go up to the beach for the weekend.'

'Oh, yes. Actually, I already said we would.'

I turned and looked at him. He had that gentle look about him and he smiled slowly at me, as slowly as the water dripping a path down my arm.

'Good. It'll do us good.'

I set down the lettuce and went over to him, put my hands against his arms and leaned close, kissed his warm cheek. I did love him.

'Shit,' he said.

I pulled away. 'What?'

'I've got a workshop on Saturday.'

'Typical.'

♪ ♪ ♪

I took the small car and drove up to the beach by myself. Michael promised to follow as soon as his workshop was finished, but I wasn't holding my breath. I knew how long those things could drag on for.

When I turned into the drive, I spotted Nick and Pamela Frewen sitting on the porch, and groaned. I hoped there would be someone more interesting than those two. I went up to the porch. Peter was in the hammock, swinging a sleeping Ellie in his arms.

'Hello!' Pete bellowed.

'Ssh! You'll wake the baby!'

'Nah, this one sleeps through anything. I won't get up, though. Lissa will get you a drink, she's in the kitchen.'

Then Adrian appeared in the doorway carrying a tray with a jug of pink grapefruit juice and glasses.

'Hi Cara. Juice?'

'Hi. Thanks, that'd be great.'

'Where's Michael?' asked Liss.

'He got held up. He's coming later tonight.'

I went inside on the pretext of visiting the bathroom. I hadn't expected Adrian. I felt flustered and wondered how Michael would get on with him. Adrian was much younger of course, and they didn't have much in common. But then, Michael would be happy talking to Pam and Nick and the others. It would be fine, as long as we could all find a bit of space to ourselves. I went into the bedroom and unpacked a few things from my bag, brushed my hair and sprayed on a little perfume before going out again.

Lissa was in the kitchen, buttering sandwiches. She looked tired.

'Ellie's a darling,' I said.

'Yes, when she's asleep. I'm still getting up twice a night.'

'You must be exhausted.'

'I'm feeling it a bit today.'

'Here, let me do that.' I poured her a glass of wine and took over the sandwiches.

'Thanks Car. I think I'm trying to do too much for this anniversary. It's like I'm trying to pretend things are just the same since the baby.'

'And they're not?'

She just looked at me and I felt myself blushing. I tried to make up for it.

'Why don't I do the cooking?'

'Don't be stupid. I didn't ask you up here to work.'

'But I'd enjoy it.'

'Well you can enjoy not doing it too. Besides, it's just a barbecue tonight. I'll chuck some lettuce in a bowl and the boys can take over and burn everything to a crisp.'

We were laughing when Adrian came in.

'Sounds like fun in here. Can I help?'

'I was just making it my new policy to say yes to all offers of help,' said Lissa, grabbing him by the shoulders and pointing him towards the fridge. 'You can be in charge of the cheeseboard.'

'Only if you promise to take your drink and go entertain the troops. Someone's got to.'

'Absolutely.' She paused and turned at the door. 'You behave yourselves.'

Adrian got out some cheeses and stood next to me at

the bench as he unwrapped them.

'Don't you believe in crusts?'

'What?'

'You're cutting off all the crusts. They're the best bits.'

I looked down at the exact triangles with their careful layers of green and red.

'I always do sandwiches like this.'

'I suppose we can give them to the chooks.'

'They're perfectly edible! They just look like they're for show.'

'I was talking about the crusts.'

'Oh.' I threw one at him. He threw one back and we giggled. He had a lovely grin.

'Go and entertain the troops yourself,' I said.

'Maybe later.'

Later turned out to be after the barbecue. Pulse had been experimenting with fire-sticks and just as everyone was getting mellow, after too much food and drink, Adrian got up and fiddled around with the barbecue. Nobody was taking much notice until suddenly he was standing among us whirling a blazing stick. He stamped all around in a semi-circle, moving the fire up and down in a blur of orange. Every now and then he'd let out a sharp yell and jump back, then stamp, stamp, stamp again. He seemed oblivious to us after a while, absorbed by the pace and light of the whirling fire-stick. It was like he was a kind of warrior. But it was the music that fascinated me. The whole thing had a definite music to it: the stamping, the shouts, the whirring of the stick and the crackle of the flames. I tried to describe it afterwards, when there was only me and Adrian and Pam left outside, watching the stars in the sky.

'It's like you can make music out of anything,' I said.

'You *can* make music out of anything,' he said.

'Not really,' said Pam. 'Not real music. It's just noises.'

'What do you think music is then?'

'I don't know. A melody, a tune.'

'That's one kind. There are lots of kinds. You just need to learn to listen. Here.'

He leapt up and grabbed a couple of bamboo sticks out of the garden, tested them against his knee and stood, looking up at the night clouds. A few moments passed before I heard it: his breath. He was breathing softly through his mouth; gradually the sound got louder until he was almost panting. I looked over at Pam. She was looking quizzical. Then Adrian raised one of the bamboo sticks and brought it down, fast. He did the same with the other one. They made a kind of whipping noise. Whip, whoosh. He did it again. Whip, whoosh. Then quicker, and quicker again, the sounds built up to a whistling crescendo, then slowed and slowed and stopped. Pam laughed and clapped, and I clapped too. I heard the sound my palms made as they slapped together, and I smiled.

♪ ♪ ♪

When we got back home on the Sunday night, Michael went and did some work in his study after dinner and I lay on the couch listening to CDs.

I wondered about the way I was feeling. Was this new happiness because of Adrian? Since he had come into my life I felt more alive. It was as if I had fallen into a rut, a routine, a way of living, or being, that was not really where I wanted to be. Adrian had made that apparent to me, so I inevitably connected him with the feeling of restlessness. But it wasn't as Michael suspected – it wasn't Adrian precipitating change. It was me. It's just a shame I didn't realise that at the time.

It started to rain, and behind the music I could hear the steady falling on the window panes and the trees outside. Hundreds of tiny tap, tap, taps. Remember, remember. I began to drift off to sleep and, somewhere between sleeping and waking, I realised. It wasn't the sound I remembered. It was the way of listening – listening through the heart.

♪ ♪ ♪

Ritenuto

I STARTED losing it. It was like I was caught up in a wind, one of those winds that meteorologists warn police about, the ones that can drive people mad. I began to think of myself as the person Adrian thought I was. That light he shone on me, I basked in it, and I began to believe myself as rich and mysterious as the shadows that spotlight lent me.

I began to see more and more of Adrian, hungry for that intense focus. At the time I usually thought it a coincidence – he'd be invited to the same functions or I'd run into him on the street and we'd end up going for dinner or a drink. Often I'd just be thinking of him, and suddenly there he was. It was a bit strange. It made it hard to escape the feeling that we were meant to be together.

And he was always fun to be with, full of tall tales which I wanted to believe. He liked it when I believed, although I think it lessened his respect for me at the same time. But he was always interested in me, asking questions, not just about my work and life, but about my opinions – what I thought of the latest artwork or film or book or piece of music he'd just discovered and become passionate over. It was his passion that magnetised me. It was extreme, and thrilling to witness. Only when that intense passion was directed towards me did it become scary.

But, in the beginning, his interest was irresistibly flattering. He would listen to me in a way that made me keep talking when usually I would have stopped. So that I was talking on past what I'd already figured out, so I was thinking as I was speaking, wondering at the back of it all where my mind was travelling. There was something exciting about that. It was like I was finding out what I thought about things at the same time he was. Adrian's approval gave my opinions validity. I shudder at that now, but at the time it filled me with a sense of success, that feeling you get when danger is overcome.

He always took me to interesting places, places I wouldn't go normally: night markets, circuses, windswept hilltops with views of my city I had never seen. And there was always the music. I heard more music than I'd ever heard in my life. That is the part I find hardest to explain. That's what started it all. Somehow that music got inside me and filled all those gaps, those little pockets of emptiness that had been there a long time, just waiting.

It was at one of the concerts that I made my decision to make the relationship more than a friendship.

We were standing in a group at the interval, sipping wine. The others were musicians too and they were all talking about the music. I enjoyed listening to them but I couldn't understand most of it: something about the pentatonic scale and some dispute over time signatures. As the bells rang for the audience to return to their seats, I asked Adrian about it. He explained that my favourite movement had been in three-four time.

'I don't really understand what "time" means,' I admitted.

'Time signatures? That's how many beats there are in a bar. Here, I'll show you.'

And he took me by the wrist and raised and lowered my hand in quick succession.

'That's two-four, one two, one two. Here's three-four time.'

And he moved my hand across in the shape of a triangle.

'You see, like in a waltz. One two three, one two three.'

And he swept an arm around my waist and waltzed me back to the auditorium doors. As we sat down in our seats and the lights lowered, I looked at him watching the stage. If he turns now and looks at me, I thought, if he turns now. He turned and smiled. And that was the decision made.

♪ ♪ ♪

About that time, Michael and I went away for a weekend. I suggested it. I don't know why. Well, yes, I do know why. It didn't work anyway. We went down the coast to one of the small towns squeezed between mountains. It rained the whole time. Man, did it rain. Buckets of it. I'm used to rain – in the city it rains a lot, a humid rain which falls sudden and hard, pelts down like someone yelling, and then eases off and is softer, quieter – but this was different. It never eased off. Maybe it did at night, when we were asleep, but otherwise it was just bucketing. We couldn't do anything; we couldn't go anywhere. It was awful. I stood at the hotel bedroom window looking out into the grey, listening to the rattling rain, like hundreds of tiny feet running away, and I just wanted to cry.

Michael was fine. He was quite relaxed about it, just lay on the bed reading his book. It was me who was upset by it. I wanted to go out, see whatever there was to see. I didn't want to be stuck in a hotel room with Michael. And yet that's why I'd suggested we went away. So why couldn't I have just lain next to him, taken that book away, and said, 'Michael, we've got to talk'? Conditions were perfect. But I guess I'm not. I had to go out.

On the corner there was a small museum, just four rooms, run by volunteers. It was all about the town's gold-mining history. It took me 20 minutes to go round all the exhibits. There were some old black and white photos at the end – pioneers with grim expressions, a few Chinese with long plaits down their backs, everyone seeking gold, the answer to all their problems. I wondered if they found what they were looking for, or if their problems just transformed into different ones.

I ran across the road in the rain and had a cup of tea at the tearooms. I thought about talking to Michael. I thought about what I would say. But putting it out there like that, whichever way I tried, it simply sounded foolish. I still loved Michael. I still wanted to be with Michael. So what was it I wanted, exactly? I wasn't sure, but I knew what I didn't want. I decided not to tell him.

I still think I made the right decision.

I went back to the hotel. I was soaking by the time I got there. I ran in the doors and paused in the foyer to catch my breath, shaking my coat on the stone floor. Michael was standing at the front desk, talking to the concierge. I looked at him, not recognising him for a moment, then I realised, of course, it was Michael. I stood for a minute, watching them talking, thinking, This is what Michael looks like to everyone else. A tall man, thick dark hair, well dressed, polite, his large hands holding an envelope gently in front of him as if it were a gift. Gentle, that's who he is, I thought. He is a gentle man. And I love him.

I went up behind and pinched his bottom, made him jump a little, smiled at the way he let his eyebrows rise only a fraction in front of the concierge. The rest of the weekend was easier. I allowed myself to relax, I guess. I allowed myself to love them both.

♪ ♪ ♪

175

When I first met Michael, I was fascinated by his job. I was always asking him questions about it. I was like a little kid interminably asking 'Why?' I thought he held the answers to everything.

I remember the second time we met, he told me all about attraction. It wasn't a ploy, I'm sure, but it worked. We were out with Lissa and Pete and while they were having their own conversation, I asked Michael about them. I was flirting indirectly; I didn't ask about myself, although I was dying to know how he saw me.

'You've known Pete for years, so tell me, why is he in love with Lissa?'

It was just a game, but Michael took it seriously. He looked over at Melissa and thought hard before he answered.

'Have you ever met Pete's mother?' he asked.

'You're kidding!' I said. 'No way is Lissa Pete's mum!'

'Well, no. But you must admit she has certain motherly qualities. Men do tend to seek that out sometimes. Men who were denied those qualities in their own mothers.'

How ridiculous, I thought. But afterwards I couldn't help thinking of Pete and Lissa like that. Maybe Pete was looking for that 'perfect mother'. And after they had Ellie, Liss told me that Pete got surprisingly jealous.

'It's like you can see inside people,' I said to Michael once.

'Not as well as you can!' he laughed.

I thought about that when I was at work, taking MRIs or CTs of the insides of people. I'd look at the skull images and imagine what electric messages were whizzing along those bright lines of connection. I must have seen pictures of brains experiencing all kinds of emotions. I wondered what love looked like. Which part of the brain lit up when you fell in love? I imagined a large heart shape lighting up inside the brain, pulsing bright red, pumping out hormones.

I liked looking inside people. Not like Michael, though. I could never tell a murderer's liver from any other sort of liver. After a while I got sick of looking at bones and damaged organs. I wanted to see things more miraculous. So I trained to specialise as a sonographer. That way I got to see a miracle almost every day.

Not every day. Occasionally women would come in and lie down anxiously, and when I dragged the ultrasound around the cool gel on their stomachs there would be no movement. No heartbeat. They didn't always realise immediately. I would have to tell them. They didn't always realise even then. Afterwards I would clean up slowly, take overly long straightening the room, and sometimes I would sit on the edge of the bed and put my head in my hands and cry.

Those times made me appreciate the normal ultrasounds, so they never became mundane. Usually both parents came along, anxious, excited, holding each other's hands. They'd get settled and I would turn on the machine and there, in the moving sea of grey, the first glimpse of their child. Such wonder. I'd have to go through it slowly. That round is the head, that circle the stomach, see those wee dots, they're fingers, see the baby's waving. Never 'he' or 'she', unless they asked. The

177

mother usually cried. Then I'd get on with the job, checking all the organs, measuring lengths, checking the cerebellum, the butterfly of the brain, heart, abdominal walls, kidney, cord insertion, diaphragm and so on.

When I went home I'd tell Michael about it. How they all had little personalities, even when only a few months old. Some were always moving, trying to get away from the ultrasound; some would yawn or suck their thumbs. The parents couldn't see them as well as I could; I was so used to delving through that magic grey sea, a professional diver looking for life underwater. I could see every little thing. I could see the line of their lips, the tips of their tiny toes.

How odd to have something growing inside you like that. How amazing. I couldn't imagine having that myself.

♪ ♪ ♪

Lento

I FELT strangely vulnerable around that time. Not just emotionally, but physically. I kept having the feeling someone was watching me. At night I'd go around checking all the locks and drawing the curtains. It didn't help that Michael was away a lot. And when he was around, he seemed preoccupied. He often gets that way when he's worried about someone – usually one of his clients. He had just taken on a couple of new clients, so I put it down to that. It always takes a while for him to figure them out, to bed them in, as it were. He puts a lot of effort into his clients. It can be very draining.

I remember now a strange phone call I got one night when Michael was working late. I thought it might be Adrian at first, but the voice sounded different and the man was reluctant to identify himself.

'Hello.'

'Hello. Is that Cara?'

'Yes.'

'Cara Wilson?'

'Yes. Who's that?'

'Oh, hello Cara. How nice to finally talk to you.'

'Who is this?'

'Michael's told me so much about you.'

'Are you a friend of Michael?'

'Yes, yes, of course.'

'I'm afraid Michael's not in at the moment.'

There was a pause.

'Oh, really?'

'Can I tell him you called?'

'No, I wouldn't like to worry him.'

There was something in his tone I couldn't place.

'He'll be home soon,' I said in a rush. 'I'm expecting him any moment. Give me your name and I'll get him to ring you back.'

'No need, no need. Just tell him . . . just tell him Vincent called.'

And he hung up. Strange, I thought. I must ask Michael about him.

But I went to bed before he got home that night and the next morning I didn't get a chance. The phone rang again and after that conversation I forgot the earlier one entirely. It was my mother.

'It's James,' she said.

'What? Has he got worse again?'

My stepfather had started suffering from angina

and mum had been worried.

'He's gone, sweetheart.'

For a minute I wondered where he'd gone. For a minute the idea flickered briefly that he'd walked out too, like Dad. But not James. James was too reliable, too kind, too constant for anything so carelessly hurtful. She meant something else.

'You mean . . . what's happened?'

'He had a heart attack late last night.'

'My God. Is he . . .'

I was going to say 'all right' but I knew before I said it that he wasn't all right.

'He's dead, my darling.'

'Oh Mum.'

I could hear her crying and imagined her standing in the hallway of her house, leaning against the little telephone table where she kept her keys and a notebook full of lists of Things To Do. There would be plenty of things to do now. How would she cope without James? It was James who had always managed things like this. I felt helpless. I said I would ring Eve and we'd come up right away.

After I hung up I sat down on the floor and tried to think of what to do. I got as far as heading up a piece of paper with 'Things To Do' before bursting into tears. Michael came in and looked shocked. He asked what was wrong and sat down beside me and I clung to him, weeping. It was a few minutes before I was calm enough to tell him. He just kept stroking my hair, rocking me.

James was, in effect, my father. It was James who

drove me and Eve to hockey at the weekends, and picked us up from school discos. It was James who gave me a stern talking-to as a teenager when I was giving mum a hard time. James was always there, organising us as a family, going to work to support us, being proud of us, listening to us.

'I can't remember if I ever told him I loved him.'

Michael patted my back. 'He knew it, Cara. And he loved you back.'

I lifted my wet face from his shoulder. I could taste salt on my lips.

'Do you know it, Michael?'

He looked at me so gently, so sweetly, that I had to press my face back into his chest.

Michael helped me get organised and cancelled my commitments for the rest of the week. I rang Eve and she said she'd come up in a couple of days. Bloody Eve. She always left it up to me to carry the family can. I remembered what mum was like when Eddie left.

Michael offered to drive me up there but I knew he had clients, so I said I'd go on my own. He could take Friday off and come up for the funeral. On the road I realised I'd forgotten to cancel a concert date with Adrian. Too bad. He'd just have to wait. I felt a secret sense of satisfaction at the idea of him waiting for me, of me not turning up. I thought about ringing him to say I was going out of town, to tell him why. But I couldn't imagine what he would say in reply. Comfort just wasn't in his repertoire. He may have helped me in some way, I suppose, just by being there. He had a way of making me feel more . . . 'grounded'. But a lot of that must have come from my idea of him, the picture I had built around the person. Was it the background picture I was in love with or was it the man? Now I think I just filled in the background with all the things I needed at the time.

It was Michael I needed. I wished I'd let him drive me up north, asked him to come with me. Bugger the clients. How would I cope with mum? She and James must have been together 20 years. I tried to imagine what it would be like if Michael died; what would I do, how would I feel? The road shimmered and blurred and I had to pull over. I sat there for half an hour, by the edge of a field, the long grass whispering in sympathy.

It turned out mum wasn't as bad as I'd thought. She even answered the door with a smile.

'I'm so glad to see you, darling. Thank you for coming.'

We hugged for a long time and I started to cry. Mum drew me inside and sat me on the couch. I leaned my face against her shoulder and she put her arm around me, as if I was a child.

'What was it like?' I asked.

'Very quick. It was a major heart attack. He had no chance of recovery.'

'But I thought he was taking drugs.'

'For angina, yes. But they couldn't have stopped this.'

She looked at me and gave me a handkerchief.

'He expected it, you know. We both did.'

'But how could you? Angina doesn't always mean a sudden heart attack.'

'I don't know. He just knew. He told me a few weeks

ago that he thought something might happen and he was organising his will and so on. We talked about it and said the things we needed to say.'

I put my hand on hers.

'He was a lovely man, Mum.'

'Yes.'

I was amazed at how calm she was. She just accepted it all, as if it was fate. James believed in fate. Maybe mum had become more like him through the years of their marriage. I remember when I was a teenager, upset over the latest doomed love affair, James would come and talk to me. He'd bring a cup of hot sweet tea to the bedroom door and knock softly. I always let him come in. Not mum, but James I would always let in. Sometimes I would tell him a bit about the boy or what had happened. Even then I was attracted by the 'wrong' types. He'd listen and say, 'Well Cara, that sounds difficult. But it mustn't have been meant to be.'

I didn't believe it. I just found it more frustrating.

'So what?' I'd say. 'It hurts.'

I can see how they found it comforting: the idea that some things were meant to happen. Some time somewhere the thing that was meant to happen would. It's very tempting, but I can't afford to believe that. We make our own destinies.

It helped mum, though. Or something did. She coped much better than I'd expected. She made all the arrangements for the funeral, the flowers, the coffin, the service. I wasn't much help at all. It made me wonder about my memory of the time Eddie left. Perhaps mum hadn't been as stricken as I remembered. Perhaps she'd just let me think I was helping. That went straight to my idea of who I was. Another thing I didn't want to think about.

It was a nice service, in a small church. About 50 people were there.

'Better by far you should forget and smile
Than that you should remember and be sad.'

That was James all right.

Michael came up for the day and sat beside me, held my hand. It was good to feel him there, standing a little behind me as the coffin was lowered into the damp ground. He placed his hand gently on the small of my back so I knew he was there. Michael was always there when I needed him.

He's like James in that way. Constant. I needed that, especially after Eddie, my real father, left. I still find it disturbing to see Eddie; he has so much restless energy. He lives out west now, with his new wife Priscilla.

'Where do you find a wife called Priscilla?' I'd asked him when he told me he was getting married again.

'The desert?' he replied, with a grin.

It used to annoy me, that grin. How could he not care? How could he not see that leaving your wife and family was a serious matter? He was always having fun, or looking for the next fun to be had. He left mum for Mary. Then he left Mary for Joanne. Now it's Priscilla. 'He has a problem with commitment, your father,' says Michael. No kidding. Last year we spent Christmas with him and Priscilla. She's okay. I like her better than the others anyway. She's more down to earth. She goes along with

185

his crazy adventures – the yachting trip around the islands, the hot-air balloon disaster – but she makes sure he faces up to the practicalities. Well, some of them. You can never get Eddie to think about all the practical details.

That Christmas, he and I stayed up late one night, watching a movie on television: *The End of the Affair*, with Ralph Fiennes and Julianne Moore. I didn't like her, she got on my nerves. Why couldn't she just follow her heart, instead of all those excuses? God – the biggest excuse of them all. But what kind of God would deny the chance of true love? Wasn't God meant to *be* love? Yet, when Eddie started criticising the plot, I defended it. It was the way he talked about love that annoyed me.

'What a waste. She should have just left that bloody fool husband.'

'Maybe she loved him.'

'Well she obviously loved Ralph, didn't she? Why didn't she just get on with it?'

'Didn't you get it at all? She'd made a vow. Some people are true to their vows.'

He usually didn't notice my digs. Or maybe he just chose to ignore them.

'Well it was a bloody stupid vow. Should you be true to your vows or true to yourself?'

Maybe he had noticed my dig. I felt a little ashamed and went to bed soon after, but couldn't sleep. I kept thinking about the movie. I'd said to Eddie that she should have been true to her vow. But it wasn't what I felt. I'd felt the same as my father – my father who had such problems with commitment. Maybe I was more like him than I knew. I didn't like the idea. Eddie may have thought he was being true to himself, but really he was just being selfish, wrecking other people's lives. I didn't want to be like that.

I couldn't help admiring Eddie in some ways, though. I admired his confidence. He was always so sure of himself, often way beyond his abilities, but that never put him off – he was always willing to give something a go. Sometimes it annoyed the hell out of me, but secretly I would applaud. Eddie was always ready to take whatever was thrown at him.

That reminds me of Adrian. He told me once that when he was drumming he always had to be ready. One of the band could yell out Take it! at any time, and he'd have to take a solo right then and there. Eddie would love that. He'd be right into it. Am I really like him? Am I ready to solo at a moment's notice?

♪ ♪ ♪

Presto

I DIDN'T cope with James's death very well. I tried to keep busy afterwards, to concentrate on work. But I wasn't feeling too good. Every time I took an ultrasound and saw the wriggling creatures on screen I felt seasick. I booked in a few more days off. Bereavement, I said. No one questioned it.

Adrian was away somewhere but kept ringing. It was almost annoying. But he'd always cajole me out of any irritation, tell me some funny story, or talk about a piece of music he was working on. Then one night he rang to announce he was back in town again.

'Come out, come out.'

'I can't, I'm too tired.'

'That's because you haven't got out enough lately. Come on, there's a new Greek restaurant which has dancing.'

I groaned. 'Just what I need. I'd rather stay home and break plates.'

'What's Michael up to?'

I didn't like him asking about Michael. I briefly considered lying.

'He's working.'

'Come out then. You don't want to stay home on your own, getting bored.'

That was the trouble. I didn't.

'If you don't want to go out, why don't you come round here and we'll get a video?'

I knew what would happen. At least, I thought I knew. Turned out I didn't know the half of it. But Adrian had never invited me round before. It was tempting. I wanted to see what his house looked like, see who he was in his own environment. So I went.

The flat was not exactly what I expected. It was untidy, with strange art on the walls, mismatched curtains and faded carpet, quite unlike the careful grooming of the man himself. Adrian went into the kitchen to make coffee and I looked around the living-room, looking for pieces of him that I could hold up and compare with what I already knew. There wasn't much, and I couldn't be sure what belonged to the two flatmates, who were out. A cluttered coffee table, a rack overflowing with magazines, tons of CDs stacked against the wall – a huge range from Brahms to Pearl Jam. Those would be Adrian's. There was a shelf stacked with books, some on music, but a surprisingly eclectic range. I hadn't realised he was much of a thinker. The room smelled of Adrian – that tobacco, that particular aftershave. I sat on the couch, waiting for him to bring me a drink, and I breathed him in.

He brought me a glass of wine and sat down next to me, talking. He was talking too fast, he was talking shit. I think he was nervous, even more nervous than later on, when we were all nervous. We were both anticipating sex.

He got up to put the video on and sat down again, not so close this time. It was a Hollywood comedy, not bad, although we never got to see how it turned out. I sat back and relaxed. It was strange but I wasn't jumpy at all. I wondered what was going to happen with a kind of distance, as if it was our story playing out on the screen.

Then at one point I went to the bathroom and looked at myself in the mirror. The woman shook her head at me with a little frown. 'Silly girl, you don't love him,' she said. Who was this woman? So collected, so confident. She looked beautiful with her big brown eyes and thick soft hair, her gold and amber necklace glinting against her tanned skin.

Where was Cara? Here was another Cara. I had found myself and lost myself all at once.

Perhaps that is what love is. Perhaps this was who I was looking for and I didn't need any more than that. I washed my hands for the second time, rubbing my palms together, listening to the splash of water against the marble basin. And I decided to leave.

When I remember the night now, I remember this part clearly. I made my decision to go before anything else happened. The rest is a blur. I have to concentrate to lift the fog, to get the order of it all, to remember things exactly as they were said. It's important to get it right, for me to remember the rhythm of the words.

It started as I walked back down the hallway and glanced into Adrian's bedroom. Just a glance. I wasn't meaning to pry or uncover. But I saw it there on the bedside table and I had to look again. Then I had to go in to double-check. It made me wonder. It made me wonder about a lot of things. That bloody photo became a kind of trigger somehow for the subsequent events. It doesn't make sense, I know, but then nothing made much sense from that point on.

When I came back into the lounge, Adrian was standing there holding out another glass of red wine. The video screen was paused behind him, a man and a woman frozen in mid-sentence, her hands raised before her as if to ward off something dangerous.

'No thanks, I better go.'

'Just one more.'

'I really don't feel like it.'

I picked up my purse, unsure of whether to ask about the photo.

'Don't go,' he said.

He stepped forward and held my hand. It didn't feel like I imagined it would. His nails were clipped short and his palm was rough: all that drum-beating I suppose. I slowly withdrew my hand, and for a moment my fingers paused on the blue vein running along his wrist and I felt his heartbeat. It was way too fast.

I headed towards the hallway but his words stopped me.

'Wait. I'll get your coat.'

Adrian went into the bedroom and I waited in the doorway, cursing myself. When he came back he stopped a few feet away and held out the coat.

'Here you are.'

'Just give it to me, Adrian.'

And I stepped forward to take it. But he pushed past me roughly and closed the door behind us.

'What are you doing?'

'I told you I didn't want you to go.'

His tone was grating. Something was wrong. He must've noticed I'd taken back the photo.

'Well, I bloody well am going.'

I went towards the door but he stood in front of me, and then I noticed the small knife, held lightly at his side.

'What the hell . . .'

'I want to talk to you before you go,' he said. He waved towards the couch with the glinting blade. I sat reluctantly, afraid he would sit next to me, afraid he would push the cold metal against me. But he seemed wary of me now and he sat down on a chair opposite. He settled the knife awkwardly in his lap, his hand curled around the handle, one finger lightly stroking it. I didn't think Adrian would seriously hurt me, but I didn't know what to believe any more. It was like the movie we were in had changed reels and we'd been transported to a different world.

'Give me back the photo,' he said calmly, too calmly.

'No, it's mine. Why the hell did you take it in the first place?'

'Because it was meant for me. Just like you are meant for me. You know it.'

'Why would I want to be with a man who threatens me with a bloody knife?'

'This?' He lifted the knife, sounding surprised. 'I'm not threatening you. I was just going to get us some cheese and crackers. You can go whenever you like.'

'Good.' I didn't believe him but I stood up, noticing my left knee wasn't working properly. 'I'll be off then, because you're sounding like a fucking psycho.'

Adrian laughed. 'That's just what Michael thought,' he said.

'What?' My voice betrayed my fear. 'What do you mean?'

'I mean your darling husband tried to have me locked up. Nearly succeeded too.'

'I wish he had,' I said, and I sat down again, my knees collapsing under me.

How the hell did he know Michael? Why hadn't Michael said anything? I felt as if a tiny bird was fluttering inside my head, banging against my skull, trying to get out. Adrian leaned forward and poured himself another glass of wine. He looked smug.

'So,' I said slowly, sorting my words, 'you've met Michael.'

'Oh yes,' he said, with that infuriating smile. 'Weekly.'

'I see.'

I didn't know what else to say. It was too bizarre to

194

take in. I sat stunned, waiting for him to explain. His stare was unrelenting.

'You don't believe me? Let's give him a call then, shall we? We might as well make a real party of it.'

He got up and went over to the phone. I noticed that he'd set the knife down on the bench while he made the call, but somehow I didn't even think about running for it. I felt quite detached from it all. It was hopeless. There was nothing I could do.

I couldn't properly hear what he was saying, but the conversation with Michael was brief.

'He's coming over.'

'I don't see what good that will do,' I said. 'We need to sort this out ourselves, Adrian.'

For a moment he looked sad.

'It's too late for that now,' he said.

I rubbed my eyes, trying to work some reality back in.

'I don't understand,' I said. 'What exactly has been going on?'

'I've been having problems,' said Adrian. 'So I sought psychiatric help. Perfectly reasonable.'

'And I suppose you didn't know the therapist happened to be my husband?'

'I found out eventually, of course. But by then it was too late.'

I doubted everything he said now. But I had to ask the obvious question.

'And does Michael know who you are?'

He laughed. 'Not in the slightest. Your husband's not a very good therapist, you know. It's quite easy to keep

195

things from him. But then, I suppose you know that.'

There was silence for a while as we sat and glared at each other. How could I ever have thought I loved this man? That was what tormented me in the days following. I had been in love with an idea, a projection. Obviously, I had been as deluded as he.

Then we heard the noise of the front door bang and Michael appeared in the doorway. I half stood up, then sat again. Michael's face was red and he was out of breath.

'Vincent!' he puffed, holding on to the door frame.

Adrian's face had gone as still as concrete.

'Vincent?' I asked.

Michael looked over at me. I tried to smile but my mouth wouldn't work.

'Are you all right?'

'Fine,' I said stupidly. 'Who's Vincent?'

Michael looked at Adrian, who grinned.

'Vincent Adrian Madden at your service,' he said.

'Adrian?' said Michael.

He looked at me, his eyes wide, and I nodded slightly.

'At last we can all sit down and talk together,' said Adrian. 'No more secrets.'

'Look, Vincent,' said Michael. 'Cara doesn't have to be here. I'm sure we'll be able to talk better without her. Let her go and you can tell me all about it.'

'I don't need to tell you about it. Do I, Michael? You already know all about it. Have you forgotten all those conversations about your wife's infidelity?'

'What?' I said, amazed.

196

'Here she is with her lover, as good as in bed with him.'

I looked at Michael, who was unmoved, and back at Adrian. His eyes were like a lizard's.

'We never –' I started, before Michael interrupted me.

'It's all right, Cara. I'm going to come and sit down now, Vincent.'

Michael came over slowly and sat down in the other chair.

'I was wrong, Vincent,' he said.

Adrian turned his stare on to Michael.

'You deceived me,' he said.

I thought I saw the knife tremble a little in his lap.

'Yes,' said Michael. 'And you deceived me. I thought you needed to face the consequences. But that's in the past. Let's talk about now. What's going on now, Vincent?'

'I'm doing you a favour, that's what's going on. I'm bringing it all out into the open so we can fight fair.'

'You feel this is a fight? A fight over Cara?'

Adrian turned and looked at me. He had a sad smile that reminded me of the Adrian I knew. Michael leaned forward a little.

'You feel angry,' he said calmly. 'And so here we are. You're holding a knife because you feel angry. Why do you feel angry, Vincent? Who are you angry with?'

'For fuck's sake, give it a rest, Michael. We're not here for therapy.'

'What are we here for?'

'We're here for Cara to make a decision.'

He pointed at me with his right hand which held the

knife. I couldn't help jumping. Adrian laughed – a harsh, barking laugh – and after a minute Michael joined in.

I was shocked. Please God, I thought. Please let us get out of this. It's all my fault. If we can just all get out of this, I'll make it right.

Michael stopped laughing a second after Adrian. I looked from one to the other, bewildered. I was almost sure Michael was trying to wink at me.

'I'm not making any decisions when there's a knife involved,' I said shakily.

'Fair enough,' said Michael.

'It's just for cheese,' said Adrian. 'But if it makes you feel better.'

He put it down on the coffee table in front of us.

♪ ♪ ♪

Tempo primo

THE NEXT day I woke up feeling sick. Some sort of flu bug, I thought. Then I remembered. I got out of bed and ran to the bathroom. It was a little better after I threw up.

Michael told me to stay in bed. I needed to recover, he said. I took his advice, and he went to meet a colleague to make arrangements for transferring Adrian to a new therapist. Michael wasn't sure he would go, but it was worth a shot, he said.

Every time the phone rang I wondered if it could be Adrian, but it wasn't.

The following day I was still feeling ill. Every time I closed my eyes I kept thinking about it all. I stayed in bed again and tried to distract myself by reading a trashy novel. Michael came home early and made me chicken soup. He was worried about me.

'We've got to talk,' he said. 'Are you afraid he's going to bother you again?'

'No.'

'There's no guarantee, I suppose. But I'm doing my best to get him the help he needs. I can't get him locked up this time.'

'I know. It doesn't matter. Honestly, I don't think he's going to be a problem any more.'

Despite Michael's warnings about anti-social personality disorders, I really didn't think Adrian would try anything again. I had only to remember the shock on his face, the uncharacteristic vulnerability that came over him as we'd left.

'What are you afraid of then?' asked Michael.

'Myself, I suppose.'

He was shocked. 'You can't blame yourself,' he said. 'You had no idea how he was manipulating us all.'

'That's not really the point,' I said.

'Well, would you like some counselling? I can arrange for one of my colleagues to see you today.'

'No. Thanks. I'm not feeling upset emotionally, more physically ill.'

'Physical illnesses often have emotional causes.'

'I know. But honestly, emotionally I feel fine. I feel like . . . something has settled in me, something has clicked into place.'

Michael looked bewildered.

'I'm going to take a few days off to look after you,' he said.

'Don't be silly, I'm fine. Your clients need you more

than I do. I'll be all right by tomorrow.'

But I wasn't. Michael stayed home with me, and I wished I could be the one looking after him. He made me promise to go to the doctor.

It's probably stress, she said, or it could simply be a virus, or even food poisoning. I should get some rest.

I had another couple of days in bed but by the time Monday rolled around I wasn't much better.

'I think we should talk more about it,' said Michael.

'I don't need to talk about it. I'm ill,' I said.

Michael dropped me at the doctor's again on his way to work. Blood tests, she said. We'd better check you out properly.

I sat in the nurses' room, waiting for someone to come and take my blood, and I wondered what they would find floating around in me. It wasn't that I was sick, I decided. It was that I was recovering. Maybe they would see large prickly white cells attacking little heart-shaped red ones. I was just getting Adrian out of my system.

They ran some tests – nothing. Stress, they said again; perfectly understandable. I made them run some more. This time the nurse phoned.

'I think you'd better come in,' she said.

'Can't you tell me over the phone?'

'Well . . . I really think you'd better come in.'

What the hell was so bad they couldn't tell me over the phone? I started to get worried. If this crisis had affected me physically, maybe the guilt had literally got to me. Except that I didn't have anything to feel guilty about, according to Michael.

By the time I got in there, I was convinced I had cancer. Could they tell that from a blood test? I didn't think so. Even so, I started thinking about my will, planning my own funeral. They kept me waiting 20 minutes. I was dying and I was wasting precious time in a waiting room. My hands started to sweat and itch.

'Cara Wilson.'

I followed the doctor into her room and sat on a chair.

'Just tell me quickly,' I said.

She sat down and smiled at me. She sure wasn't used to telling people they were going to die.

'Just tell me,' I said. 'How long have I got?'

'About seven and a half months,' the doctor said, still smiling.

So short. How would I do all the things I wanted to do in that time?

'You're pregnant,' she said.

♪ ♪ ♪

I waited outside the building for him. I didn't want to go in. I didn't like asking for him, waiting for him in front of people. Besides, it was a beautiful day. There was no wind to speak of and the sun played on my bare arms. I hugged them to myself and felt their warmth and hummed a little under my breath. I remembered: this was what it was to be happy.

When I opened my eyes he was standing in front of me, smiling. He leaned forward and kissed me on the lips softly.

'Hello,' he said.

'Hello.'

'I've brought a picnic.'

We walked down the street and up some steps, round the back of one of the government buildings and into the old cemetery. We held hands as we walked. They were a little sticky in the heat but I liked it; it made me feel young again. I pretended we were university students with nothing else to do, no one else to think of, wandering through the gardens. We walked up the bridge across the motorway, the cars buzzing past under our feet, past the jagged rows of crooked headstones, through into the park beyond. There was a huge green tree with red flowers offering shade in a corner, and he steered me towards it. He'd brought everything in a hamper, even a small travel-rug, and he spread it out under the tree and got out some drink and cheese and bread and tomatoes.

We lay on our backs next to each other and looked up through the tree branches. The odd flash of crimson broke through the deep green. Michael turned on his side towards me and reached out his hand. I took it and closed my eyes, placed his hand on my stomach, hearing the hum of the sky, my breath in and out, the rhythm of my heartbeat. It was slow and steady, as constant as a metronome.

♪ ♪ ♪